THE MYSTERY AT WICKENBURG

Gary T. Brideau

THE MYSTERY AT WICKENBURG

iUniverse books may be ordered through booksellers or by contacting:

iUniverse
1663 Liberty Drive
Bloomington, IN 47403
www.iuniverse.com
1-800-Authors (1-800-288-4677)

ISBN: 978-1-5320-9509-2 (sc)
ISBN: 978-1-5320-9510-8 (e)

Print information available on the last page.

iUniverse rev. date: 02/12/2020

My thanks to my sister, T. Jene Brideau,
Who started me writing and kept me going.

Bruce and his wife Sylvia move to Wickenburg, Arizona to start a ranch. Silvia doesn't like the idea of living in a sandbox as she refers it too but goes along with her husband. shortly after the ranch is underway life looked good. However, someone has set their desires for that same property to make a lot of money and tries to force Bruce off his land by giving him all kinds of trouble.

CHAPTER 1

A WOLF IN THE FOLD

Bruce, a man 30 years old with dark brown hair, pulled his silver SUV to the side of the road outside of Wickenburg, Arizona. Pointed to the barren piece of land, and said to his wife Sylvia, a 30-year-old woman who is 6' feet tall with a perky figure, and short brown hair, "My Love, this is where we are going to live. I purchased eight hundred acres of this stuff. I figure, we can raise some cattle, and a few chickens, and set up enough wind turbines, to turn a profit."

Sylvia stared at the bleak wasteland, and questioned, "Bruce. Where is the grass, and the, trees like there are in Tennessee? All I see is one big, sandbox."

"Give it a chance, and it will grow on you."

"That›s what I am afraid of."

"Say what?"

"Just skip it," grumbled Sylvia.

Bruce grinned sheepishly, and reported, "I can›t get my money back so we're stuck, with an eight-hundred-acre litterbox."

Sylvia stared at her husband, smiled, then gave him a kiss on the lips saying "There is more, where that came from. Just wait until we get back to the motel. Now, let's get out of the car, kneel and give this land to the Lord."

While the couple was kneeling on the sand praying, a deadly scorpion stung Sylvia on her left leg. She smashed it with her hand and finished praying with her husband. Some 20 minutes later, Silvia stood and stated, "Sweetheart, no weapon that is formed against us shall prosper, that scorpion that just bit me, did not affect me. now let's celebrate."

As the month slowly passed, the ranch took shape, and Bruce carried his wife over the threshold, of their new log-cabin home. Then, with all the enthusiasm of a little girl in a candy store, Sylvia asked, "Can you give me the grand tour, of the place?"

"I thought, you didn›t like living in a sandbox?"

Sylvia slipped her arms around her husband›s neck, and stated softly, "You›re my husband, and I promised for better or worse. I figure, it's bound to get better sooner or later. Now, how about that tour?"

Halfway through the tour, Bruce stopped, turned to his wife, and questioned, "We have only been married a few months, and I still have a problem getting used to your positive attitude. And, it›s called a corral, not a cow pen. Okay, on to the bunkhouse, where some of the hired hands will be staying."

Inside the bunkhouse, Bruce introduced his wife to the men, and asked, "Harry: a 35-year-old man, 5 foot nine inches tall with short blonde hair with a van dike asked, "How are the solar panels coming along?"

"We should be finished today, and the wind turbines will be arriving tomorrow. I'll have Stubs, Ted, Andy, and Joe in the field, to get things ready for tomorrow."

Bruce turned to Sylvia, and inquired, "Do you mind going back to the house by yourself? There are a few loose ends I need to talk to Harry about."

Sylvia took her husband aside and whispered, "Pray tell why did you hire Harry. Alexis's old flame?"

"After Harry lost his wife he needed a job to help him get back on his feet."

"I was going to invite Alexis here for a month. But with him here I don't think I can. Thanks a lot."

"Don't worry it'll work out, talk to you later."

On her way back, Sylvia fantasized about having a rose garden, and flowers around the ranch house. When she passed the barn, one of the workers named Randy, a short man with short black hair stopped her, and said, "Your husband is going to be busy all day. What do you say, we have some fun?"

"Get lost Jerk, and don›t bother showing up for work, tomorrow. I will not have something like you working on this ranch."

Randy grabbed Sylvia, dragged her into the barn, and threw her on the hay. Sylvia trembled in fear then stated, "You are so dead Randy." and tried to stop him from assaulting her.

But, before Randy could do anything, Harry charged in the barn, seized him by the back of his shirt, pulled him off Sylvia, and landed a hard right cross, to his chin, knocking him down. Randy rose to his feet, saying, "Don't blame me that Trollop forced herself on me!"

Sylvia made herself decent, as Harry screamed, in rage, "She what? Mrs. Sylvia is a fine upstanding woman of God and wouldn't even think of cheating on Bruce. You have just two minutes to get off this ranch!"

As Randy passed Sylvia, he made a snide remark, Harry overheard it, and lost it and screamed as he hammered Randy's face with his fist. Bruce ran in the barn to comfort his wife, while three ranch hands: Martin, Sid, and Herb, pulled Harry off of Randy.

Bruce saw the shattered look on his wife›s face, trying to cover herself. Then slowly walked up to Randy, and stated, "You can thank your lucky stars, that I didn›t catch you, attacking my wife. Because, they would have had to take you, away in a body bag. Now, get off my property, before, I forget that I am a Christian, and do something, I›ll regret later."

Randy muttered to Sylvia, as he passed her, "Sooner or later, I will get what I want from you."

Harry, grabbed a pitchfork, rammed it in Randy›s thigh saying, "You come within a mile of Sylvia, and you›re a dead man."

Randy stared at Bruce and smirked, "What›s the matter, you too yellow to fight your own battles?"

Bruce approached Randy, swiftly brought his knee up, sending him to the ground in pain. he then, stated, "Harry, call 911, to get this garbage off my property."

With all the men gone, Bruce closed the barn doors, lay in the hay with his wife.

That evening after dinner, Bruce stared at his wife, and inquired, "Are you alright Sweet? You›ve been quiet all evening."

"It›s gonna take time for me to get over what almost happened today. But, that›s what the Lord Jesus is for."

"There›s a bit of a chill in the air. How about, if I make a fire in the fireplace, and we cuddle up?"

"I was just about to suggest that. I›ll get that big dog pillow you bought for the dog, that we don›t have, and lock the doors."

Early the next morning, Sylvia woke on the floor by the fireplace, kissed her husband, saying, "Thanks for a wonderful night. Now, if you will excuse me, I have to put something on before I make breakfast for us.'

"You look fine just the way you are, Sweet."

You wouldn›t be saying that if Harry came through that door and caught me dressed like this."

After breakfast, Bruce stood on the front porch drinking his coffee, when Harry rushed up to him, and reported, "I just checked the solar collectors, somebody threw black paint all over them, last night. That›s gonna set us back with setting up the wind generators."

"See what you can do. In the meantime, start up the backup generator. I›m going into town, is there anything you need from Bashas› store?

"How about we build a nice gazebo, for barbeques and the like?" stated Harry;

"Great idea Harry. I›ll stop by true Value Lumber and order what we need."

On the way to town, Sylvia asked, "Can we stop in at the Horseshoe Cafe for lunch?"

"I don›t see why not."

Later on that day inside the cafe, Bruce excused himself from the table and went to the men's› room. When he returned, Randy was sitting at the table trying to convince Sylvia that he could show her a good time. Bruce tapped his shoulder and said, "Do you mind. My wife and I are trying to have a peaceful lunch."

Randy pushed Bruce aside, saying, "Bug off. Can›t you see, I›m talking to the lady."

A heavyset man behind the counter bellowed, "Take it outside!"

Randy got in Bruce's face, and said, "You and me." and left."

During lunch, Sylvia stared at her husband, wondering if she married a coward, instead of a man, but, kept silent. On the way back in the SUV, Sylvia stated, "Alright mister. Out with it."

"Out with what?" questioned Bruce in mock innocence.

"You know very well what. I›ve watched you working around the ranch, and you›re not afraid of anything. But, when it comes to facing a spineless creep, like Randy, you back down. Why?"

"I have my reasons."

Halfway down the dirt road to the ranch, Bruce spotted Randy›s pickup across the road and slammed on the brakes. He got out, and demanded, "Move your truck Randy."

He leaned against the front fender of his truck, and said, "You and me. Here and now.

"Don›t be a pain in the butt. Just move your pickup."

Randy stood up, took a fighting stance, and said, "When I›m finished with you. Your wife is coming with me." He then belted Bruce in the face. He shook it off, and said, "Don›t do this Randy."

Randy laugh, and hammered Bruce›s face with his fists, sending him to the ground then went for Sylvia. Bruce heard Sylvia scream, rose to his feet, squared his shoulders, then drove his fist into Randy›s chest. Picked him up, carried him to his truck, and slammed him down on top of the hood. Randy kicked Bruce, sending him stumbling to the ground. Bruce did a backflip, and slammed his fist into Randy's face several times, before landing a few roundhouse kicks to his chest. Randy fell to the ground, stumbled to his feet, only to meet Bruce's fist. He drew his fist back for one last blow, Sylvia touched his arm, and said, "I think he's had enough."

Randy took a butterfly knife from his pocket, to kill Sylvia, Bruce stepped in the way, and caught the knife in his side, Bruce pulled it out, threw it to the ground, screamed, and knocked Randy out. He then staggered four feet, stumbled, and fell to the ground, Sylvia sat next to him, cradled her dying husband in her lap, and prayed, "Lord Jesus, help us. Took the cell phone, to call for help, but, it was a dead zone.

Bruce inquired, "Can you help me, to the SUV, and drive me to the ranch?"

Sylvia put her arm around her husband›s waist: put him in the vehicle, then moved Randy›s truck before driving to the ranch.

As soon as the SUV stopped in front of the house, Harry knew something was wrong, and shouted, "James, Stubs, Bob! Help me get Bruce in the house, then call 911."

Sylvia stayed by her husband›s side, and explained, "Randy tried to pick a fight with Bruce, but, he wouldn›t fight him. When Randy dragged me out of the SUV, Bruce kicked the crap out of Randy. He then tried to kill me with his knife but Bruce took it instead, and he sent Randy end over end before landing on the ground out cold."

"Where is Randy now?"

"Lying by his pickup on the dirt road to our ranch."

Harry asked, "Stubs. When will the ambulance get here?"

"I can›t get through. All I get is a busy signal."

"Get some men and bring Randy and his truck, here."

"Shortly after Stubs left, a tall thin man dressed in green spandex, walked in the ranch house, and inquired, "Did someone here call for help?"

"Yes. My husband is in the bedroom, dying from a knife wound."

The man entered a colonial style bedroom, glanced at Bruce, and said, "I'll see what I can do. But, I can't be disturbed."

"Three hours later, the man shook Sylvia›s hand, saying, "You are fortunate that I was passing by, or, your husband would be dead right now."

"What do I owe you?"

"Nothing, my lady. Just, give your husband plenty of rest." The man kissed Sylvia›s hand, and bowed, saying, "It has indeed been a pleasure meeting you, my lady." and left.

Harry stared at the man as he left, saying, "Whoa! Who let him out of the funny farm?"

The next morning, a heavy-set woman in her mid-thirties pounded on the screen door, and hollered, "Anybody to home?"

Sylvia greeted her and asked, "Can I help you?"

"I›m Clara, Harry›s older sister. He told me, that you needed help. So, here I am. Before I start to work we have to get a few things straight. As long as I›m here things will be done my way and if I don›t like something I am going to let you know it."

Sylvia stared at Clara wondering what to say when she burst out laughing, gave Sylvia a bear-hug saying, "Come here. I›m just pulling your leg. All I want you to do is rest up from your harrowing ordeal, I›ll do the rest."

"Thank you. The guest room is down the hall to your left."

Sylvia tended to her sleeping husband, poured herself a cup of tea, and sat on the front porch, that went the length of the house. Ten minutes later, Clara sat next to Sylvia with a cup of coffee, and stated, "I just saw your blood-soaked skirt you were wearing. You want to talk about it, woman to woman?"

"I›m beginning to think, that moving to Arizona, was a really bad idea."

"Did you pray about this move?"

"That was the first thing Bruce and I did. Then when the Lord opened the door we left Tennessee for here. Things went along fine at first, then, everything began to go wrong."

"Trust me, when, I say, you and your husband did the right thing. But, what else is inside you?"

"We just celebrated a year of marriage, and I thought, I had Bruce all figured out, until yesterday."

"You want to elaborate on that?"

"As long as I have known Bruce, he always let people push him around. A few weeks after I met Bruce, we were at the local diner on a date, when

Dave walked up to our booth and sat next to me. Then I spent the rest of the evening trying to keep Dave's hands away from my chest. All Bruce did was sat and watched. I figured he may be a spineless jellyfish but he›s all mine. But, yesterday Bruce shocked me when he kicked the snot out of Randy. Then, on the way back to the ranch, Bruce told me that he is a master in the martial arts, but, because he accidentally killed his opponent during a match, he swore that he would never fight back."

"Does it bother you that Bruce is a master in the martial arts?"

"No, not at all. Matter a fact, I like it."

The church in town has a twelve-step program that meets on Thursday, night. Maybe you should attend, so, you can get through this thing with Randy."

Sylvia looked Clara in her eyes, and stated firmly, "The twelve-step program was not nailed to the cross for my sins, Jesus was. So, when Jesus said, ‹it is finished,› my Healing, Deliverance, Protection, everything was provided for me, through the shed Blood of Jesus Christ on the cross. It is one step to the cross, not twelve. Anything else is dead works."

CHAPTER 2 INNER TURMOIL

The next morning while it was still dark, Sylvia rolled over in bed, kissed her husband, then got up to turn on the light, but, it wouldn›t work. Thinking that the switch was broken, she walked down the hall, through the living room, and stood on the front porch. She then made her way to the barn, saddled her Pinto, and rode off. As soon as she rode a few yards, she woke up. Then muttered, "Lord that was an embarrassing dream." Feeling insecure, Sylvia rolled over, placed her head on her husband›s chest and went back to sleep.

The next morning, Bruce, rubbed his wife›s thigh saying, "Hey, Sweet Cheeks, it looks like you›re stuck with me for a few more years."

"How do you feel?"

"Like a southbound freight-train hit me."

Sylvia whispered, "Alright, I won›t bug you this morning. But, as soon, as you are up, and on your feet. Well, we won›t talk about that right now. I don›t want to put ideas in your head."

Bruce held his wife around her waist, saying, "It›s too late for that."

Clara knocked on the bedroom door hollering, "You two in there! Breakfast is served and getting cold!"

Bruce quickly questioned, "Who›s that?"

"That›s Clare, Harry›s sister. Now, let me go so I can get dressed."

Sylvia put on her pink bathrobe with its lacy frills walked out into the kitchen designed like the ones in an old farmhouse and said, "Good morning Clare. What good stuff, have you cooked up today?"

"Scrambled eggs with rattlesnake meat, with two-day-old coffee." quipped Clara.

"How about, a side order of escargots sautéed in butter, instead of the rattlesnake meat?" snapped Sylvia. Her attention was suddenly diverted, by a loud crash from the bedroom. Fearing the worst, she rushed into the room and found Bruce lying on the floor, struggling to stand.

Sylvia growled, "What do you think you are doing?"

"I have too much work to do to be lying in bed. Now, help me up so I can get dressed."

"The only thing you are going to do is go back in bed." she then hollered, "Clare! Can you give me a hand with Bruce?"

With Bruce in bed eating his breakfast. Sylvia sat at the kitchen table, eating her bacon, eggs, and home-fries, she glanced up at Clara and kept on eating. After she did it a few more times. Clara said, "Okay, out with it."

Sylvia explained, "I went horseback riding butt-naked and it›s bothering me."

Clare asked slowly, "Is this something you normally do? Or was it just one of those stupid ideas you had and couldn›t help yourself?"

"No, silly. I dreamed that I was riding my horse, in the nude, and I am so, embarrassed about it."

"That›s nothing. You›re just feeling exposed about something in the real world: So, go get dressed while I take care of the dishes."

Later, Sylvia sat on the front porch drinking her tea dressed in a pale blue strapless sundress. Harry walked on the porch, took off his hat and inquired, "How›s Bruce doing ma›am?"

"Weak, but, Good. Tell me. Did you find Randy?"

"No, ma›am. He was long gone when I got there. But, don›t fret any. If he comes within a mile of you, it›ll be the last thing, he›ll ever do. By the way, did Bruce beat the snot out of Randy?"

"That›s putting it, mildly."

A pickup roared up to the house and screeched to a halt. Randy jumped out wielding a baseball bat. Hit Harry in the chest, sending him to the ground, belted Sylvia›s teacup out of her hand, and threw her down on the porch. Clara rushed out hollering, "Leave her alone!"

Randy hit Sylvia in the stomach knocking the wind out of her, placed his foot on her chest, preventing her from getting up, and said, "It's just you and me Doll, all the ranch hands are out, taking care of the wind turbines, and your husband is dead. So, it's time to finish what I started in the barn." Randy lay next to Sylvia, took her in his arm and tried to kiss her. Sylvia put her hand on his face, and said, "Wait. Let me stand, and get rid of a few things so we can do it right." She stood and inquired, "Randy, can you help me with my dress?"

As soon as he was close enough, Sylvia grabbed his shoulders, brought her knee up between his pockets, sending him down on his knees groaning in pain. As Randy doubled over, Sylvia hit him on his back as he went down. He grabbed his bat, sprang to his feet, and hit Sylvia's arm, as hard as he could. She screamed in terror, as Randy kicked her in the stomach. Sylvia screamed for help, as she tried to crawl away, Harry staggered to his feet, and shouted, "Hey, Dirtbag! Leave Mrs. Sylvia alone!"

Randy spun around, walked up to Harry, and growled, "You want some more of the same?"

Sylvia, stood up, ready to jump on Randy›s back, when he hit her in the stomach, with the butt of the bat, then landed an uppercut to her jaw, sending her flying backward, on the porch. Harry, took hold of the bat, yank it out of Randy's hands while the ranch hands charged the porch, ready to kill Randy. He quickly took a nine-millimeter gun from the inside of his shirt, pointed it at Harry, and ordered, "Back off you bunch of Losers or Harry gets it in the head."

The ranch hands slowly raised their hands and backed away. Randy reached down, took Sylvia by the arm saying, "She is coming with me."

Bruce bellowed from the doorway, "Hey dead man, it's time to introduce you to some new pain."

When Randy took a swing at him, Bruce grabbed the bat in mid-swing and snapped it in half. Glanced down, at his battered, wife lying unconscious on the ground, and thought she was dead. Broke off one of the porch posts and said, "Batter up." and took a swing at Randy. He dove for the ground, as the beam grazed his head, hitting a porch post.

Randy screamed, "He›s gonna kill me. Somebody, do something!" he then dove for the ground again as Bruce took another swing at his head. He rolled, sprang to his feet, and jumped in his truck, to escape. Bruce leaped on the hood of the truck, drove his fist through the windshield, and hauled Randy out, whimpering. Bruce slowly drew back his fist ready to end Randy's life, when he heard, "Sweet, He's not worth going to jail."

Bruce looked down at his wife smiling up at him, trying to maintain her modesty, he then looked at Randy and dropped him on the ground. Bruce jumped off the truck got in Randy's face, and said, "You›re alive, because, my wife pleaded for you. However, you see those twelve men, each one of them looks to Sylvia as their sister."

Harry took off his shirt, put it around Sylvia›s shoulders to cover her, and said, "Boys. Let›s show what we do to an unwanted guest."

Bruce took Sylvia in his arms, walked back to the house, and vowed, "First thing tomorrow. I›m going to the bank and sell the ranch."

Sylvia stopped, looked her husband in his eyes, and said, "No. This is your dream, and I will not let you walk away in defeat, because, of some Lowlife."

Bruce stared at her and said, "You know, Mrs. Birdson you're showing more than you should. Are you hinting to me about something?"

"I don›t hint, about things like that, I›ll come right out and say that I want it. Oh, thanks for beating the snot out of Randy."

Bruce put his arm on his wife›s shoulder, Sylvia winced in pain and said, "Be careful of my arm, it hurts."

"Why don›t you sit on the porch while I get Doc."

With all the men gone back to their jobs except Harry, Bruce helped Clara to her feet, and asked, "Any broken bones?"

"No, just sore."

"Rest here. The doc will be along, soon."

Harry escorted Randy with a bloody nose, black eye, swollen lips, and multiple bruises, up to the porch. Harry nudged him and said, Randy, has something to say. Don›t you!"

Randy wiped the blood from his lip, and said, "I am sorry for assaulting you, Mrs. Birdson."

Bruce stared at Harry, and inquired, "What happened to him?"

"A pile of lumber fell on top of him," quipped Harry giving Randy a shove.

"Tie him up, until the police come for him. Harry, you look like you are in pain."

"I think I have a few busted ribs. No biggy."

"You›re a tough bird, aren›t you?"

Harry glanced at the bat, the busted porch post and queried, "You wanna tell me how you were able to snap a baseball bat in two, like a twig?"

"I don›t know. But, I do know that my wife is going to learn, how to defend herself against idiots, like Randy."

"You need to teach your wife not to throw herself at everything that has pants. Then you won›t have any problems," muttered Randy.

Harry stated, "You don't know when to shut up, do you. Here, let me show you how to keep quiet." and kicked Randy in the head, knocking him out. Harry looked up at Bruce, smiled and said, "There, that's more like it."

Hours later, Sylvia cuddled close to her husband, stared at the patrol car, as it took Randy away, and prayed that she would not have to deal with him, again. But, all that night, Sylvia Was bombarded with thoughts of Randy attacking her. The next morning, she, froze as she felt a hand gently rubbing her stomach, and thought, oh no, what is Randy doing in bed with me? This can't be happening. What am I going to do? Panic-stricken, Sylvia screamed, "Get away from me!" and jumped out of bed to escape.

Bruce stated, "Sweet, it›s me. Calm down. Randy is nowhere near you."

Sylvia climbed back in bed, cuddled close to her husband, and said, "I keep thinking that I am going to see that Creep every time I turn around."

"Why are you trembling, Sweet?"

"I am scared out of my mind that one day Randy is going to rape me," Sylvia then broke-down sobbing uncontrollably.

"I think it is time we used the motor home parked on the side of the house."

"Can we go tomorrow?"

"Sure, but, you›ll have to wear jeans instead of a dress."

"Great, I›ll pack right after we take a shower then I›ll help you get the food."

After breakfast, Bruce stated, "Clara, my wife and I are going camping for a couple of weeks. Would you mind staying a little bit longer?"

"Not at all."

After some last-minute instructions to Harry, they were on their way for some rest and relaxation at Forked Pine Campground, Southeast of Flagstaff, Arizona. Bruce, parked the motor home facing east, towards Ashurst Lake. Then, said, "This is where we are going to be for the next three weeks."

Sylvia inquired, "Sweet. Who else will be camping while we are here?"

"Just you, me, and an empty campground."

"So, I can relax in my undies without having to worry about a lot of people showing up?"

"Yup."

Sylvia took off her jeans, blouse, and shoes, put them in the bedroom, picked up a book, and said, "I am going to sit in this motor-home in my undies, for the next three weeks, reading a science fiction book called "RETURN TO ROSWELL.›"

"That›s fine with me."

That evening after Bruce went to bed, Sylvia put down her book, and searched for her thermos of hot tea. Then, remembered, "Dang, I left it on the table outside." She opened the door, poked her head out, and shown a light on the red thermos sitting on the table. Not wanting to wake her husband to get her clothes, Sylvia thought, the campground is void of campers, the grounds, are dark which means no one is going to see me. She slowly pushed the door open, stepped outside in her underwear, enjoying the cold night air for a moment, before walking to the table for her thermos of hot tea. Praying that no one would catch her in her skivvies. At her destination, she picked up, the thermos and poured herself a cup of tea. Then, muttered, I better not terry, just in case a stray camper comes by and sees me like this. She then heard footsteps behind her and softly whimpered, "Oh Lord, what do I do now?" She calmly took a sip of her tea. Sylvia›s heart pounded as she dropped her mug horrified over what she thought was going to happen next. Bruce commented, "Feeling daring tonight, I see."

Sylvia turned around, and screamed, "Why don›t you warn a body instead of scaring the crap out of me like that!"

"Sorry. But what are you doing outside dressed like that?"

Sylvia bent down, picked up her mug, wiped it out and poured herself another cup saying. "I figured, there was no one around for miles, so, I walked outside, for my tea."

"What if someone came by and saw you?"

"I›m sorry, Sweet. All I thought about was getting a cup of tea." Sylvia stared at her husband and said, "Talk about the pot calling the kettle black, what are you doing outside Dressed like that?" Sylvia paused, quickly glanced around, and asked, "What was that?" then ran inside, squealing.

The next morning, Bruce questioned, "So, Nature Girl. What are you going to do for an encore?"

"Not a repeat of last night that›s for sure. After breakfast, I›m gonna read for a bit, then walk around."

Bruce quipped, "Remember to put some clothed on before you go outside and, don›t get lost."

"Very funny."

That afternoon Sylvia picked up a bottle of water, then walked east, talking to the Lord, and not paying attention to where she was going and came to a rocky slope. Sylvia scanned the area and muttered, "Dang, I think, I›m lost."

A female voice stated "Nope. All you have to do is turn around and walk west and you'll bump right into your camper."

Sylvia stared at the diminutive woman sitting on a rock and said, "Jade what are you doing here when you are supposed to be in jail?"

"Whatever, I'm not going to argue over semantics,"

"Would you like some of my water?"

"Sure," Jade drank some, then poured half the bottle over her head saying, "Thanks. That felt good. I forgot my water."

Sylvia stared at her bottle and growled, "I don›t believe it. My delusion of Jade just used half my water."

Jade shouted, "Hey Patrick, Alexis! I found her!"

A leprechaun walked up behind Sylvia and said, "Top of the morning to ya. Lassie"

Sylvia cried, "Oh Lord, It›s Patrick. Getaway from me! Please Lord, help me. I don't want any more of this illusion."

Patrick sat on the ground with Alexis, six feet in front of Sylvia, placed his King James Bible on the ground in front of him, and inquired, "Now Sylvia, tell me, what has your insides tied up in a knot?"

Sylvia glanced at Alexis, then at Patrick and Jade commented, "By the grace of the Lord Jesus Christ, I am fine and I am not hallucinating."

"No, you are not," answered Patrick, "You›re pensive."

Sylvia moved closer to Patrick and said, "I'm an overcomer in Jesus Christ and this illusion because of the scorching heat is going to disappear."

Patrick then stated, "Something happened recently to you, that has you on the edge of your emotions. What happened?"

Now sitting next to Patrick, Sylvia realized that he was real, hung her head and explained, "I'm married to a wonderful husband, and as you know we moved out here to Arizona, from Tennessee. Everything was going great until this guy by the name of Randy, tried to assault me, a couple of times. Fortunately, he was stopped before he could, you know." Sylvia screamed, "I can't get what he tried to do to me out of my mind! Please help me! I'm afraid that I am going to lose it if it keeps up!"

Patrick placed his hand on Sylvia›s shoulder, and stated, "When, something like that, happens to a person, it is alright to feel hurt, and violated. But, you need to get past those feelings, by going to the Cross of Jesus Christ."

Alexis sat on Sylvia›s right and asked, "Can I pray for you?" Alexis placed her hand on Sylvia›s forehead and prayed for the peace of Jesus, and Sylvia was overwhelmed by Christ›s presence, fell back, and went to sleep.

Forty minutes later, Sylvia woke, stared at Alexis and Patrick, and said, "You two still, here? Anyways, Thank you for everything."

"Patrick questioned, "How do you feel?"

"Like a heavyweight has been lifted off me."

"Good. Alexis, Jade and I will see you safely, back to your camp. Then, we›ll be by, tomorrow around dinnertime."

Alexis handed Sylvia a photo of her and Patrick, saying, "Here is a little something, to remember us by."

Sylvia asked, "What are you three doing in Arizona and why is Jade out of jail?"

"It is a long story that goes like this. I walked on Alexis's deck one morning saying, "Morning me Firefly, how about a cup of hot chamomile tea And some scones?"

Alexis knelt, gave me, her Sweetest warm hug and kiss and asked, "Have I told you lately that I love you?"

"You said that just yesterday but don't stop telling me."

Alexis Put a plate of English biscuits and a stainless steel pot of hot herbal tea on the picnic table set down and ask, "What does his highness King Duncan want us to do?"

I took a bite of my scone and stated, "We are to break Jade out of jail."

Alexis's eyes bulged and almost choked on her coffee and asked, "He wants us to do what?"

At AM we met Bruce at Uncle Miltie's diner for further instructions. Later, in the diners parking lot, two men with beards and jeans rushed up to Alexis one of them whispered make it look like you're being severely beaten. Then the two men pummeled her leaving her on the parking lot crying in pain. We rushed her to the emergency room. Alexis reported to the doctor, "Two men beat me with a rubber hose and I have no feeling in my legs."

After the CAT scan Alexis Lay on the bed in an exam room, Dr. Rappaport entered, showed her the CAT scan of her back and said, "Your spinal column has been severed and there's nothing we can do." He then brought in a maroon power chair and said complements of the hospital ma'am use it in good health. Oh, and here are the keys to a white Ford van that is in the parking lot also complements of the hospital." The doctor helped Alexis in the power chair, she sat Patrick on her lap and headed for the van. However, Alexis was fine and the power chair had a secret compartment underneath.

when we arrived at the jail I distracted the guards Jade crawled into the secret compartment and we snuck her out without anybody realizing what had happened. now we have to find Jade a place to live without being falsely arrested again."

CHAPTER 3 QUANDARY

Sylvia was up early the next morning, cooked breakfast of ham and cheese omelet, with home-fries, coffee, and toast, had it on the table before, Bruce's eyes open. She then bellowed, "Come, and get it while, it's hot!"

Bruce staggered out of the bedroom in his PJ bottoms, blurry eyed and asked, "Who wound you up, this morning? After last night, I'd a thought, you would be tired this morning."

"I don't have time for that, eat your food because, we have a lot of cleaning to do."

"Hey, wait a minute. We are on vacation, which mean, rest, relax and do nothing, for the duration." grumbled Bruce.

"Sorry for the change of plans, Sweet, but, we have company coming this afternoon, and I want everything, looking spotless."

Bruce held his wife in his arms, and inquired, "What happened to you? You've been down in the mouth after Randy attacked you. Now you are a ball of energy."

"That's because I got rid of a lot of emotional baggage." She gave Bruce a kiss, and said, "Eat your breakfast."

"Aren't you going to eat?"

"I'm having a couple of eggs, sausages, toast and tea."

Sylvia sat across from her husband, put her hand in her pocket, and took out the photo of Alexis and Patrick, muttering, "They are actually coming."

Bruce was barely finished eating, when Sylvia took his plate, saying, "No time for poking around, get dressed, and make the bed, while I wash the dishes. Then, we clean every inch of our motor home, inside and out."

"Do you mind if I finish my coffee before we start chasing our tails."

Sylvia looked across the table, at her husband, and said, "I am sorry for being so energetic, this morning but I want to make a good impression on our guest."

"Can you tell me why they are coming?"

"No, all he said that he would be here for dinner."

"Do you know where he is from?"

"They are from Tennessee."

"What you are telling me is you went out, into the desert met some strange guy, who handed you a line now, you are inviting him to dinner? What happened yesterday? Or, do I want to know?"

"Nothing happened between us. He just wants to help me."

"It sounds like he wants more than just help you if you ask me."

"You have it all wrong."

"Oh, do I? I have a hard time believing you when I found you on the porch, with Randy."

Sylvia paused to control her temper, reached across the table, held her husband's hand and stated, "Sweet, you are the only one I gave myself to, and only you. When I dated Joshua he took from me what he wanted. I am sorry for not telling you the whole story. Yesterday in the desert, I turned around, and there was Alexis sitting on a rock. She called her boyfriend over and he prayed for me concerning what happened, with Randy. For some reason, he wants to talk to the both of us."

"Then you're not thinking on leaving me for some guy? It will be good to see Alexis and Patrick after all these months."

"No, the thought of leaving you never entered my mind, and I haven't a clue why Randy keeps stalking me. I never did anything to encourage him."

"I know why Randy is after you. You are a knockout when it comes to looks, and charm."

Sylvia held Bruce in her arms, and said, "Let's go back to bed and cuddle for a couple of hours. Because, it looks like my man, needs some reassurance."

The clock struck three-thirty in the afternoon, Sylvia woke with Bruce snuggled up to her side, and hollered, "Oh my gosh! Patrick and Alexis will be here any minute! Bruce you straighten up the bedroom, and I'll do a quick job on the dishes."

"How about if we get dressed first, then we can close the door on the bedroom, so they don't see the mess, then I'll fire up the grill, for the hot-dogs and hamburgers."

Sylvia had finished cleaning, took the meat out of the cooler, and was about to go outside when Bruce asked, "Aren't you forgetting something, Sweet?"

"No, what?"

"Passion pink bikini undies look great on you, but, I don't think, it will impress our company."

Sylvia smiled sheepishly and said, "Here, take this, I'll get dressed, while you greet them."

Later, she sat in a chair under the awning, clad in a large blue flowered dress. Her husband sat next to her, and inquired, "When did you say, they were coming?"

"They should be here soon. Oh ah, did you make a pot of coffee?"

Bruce looked up and watched an ATV approaching, and asked, "Is that them?"

"It sure is."

When Patrick and Alexis stepped out of the vehicle Bruce muttered,

"Hollywood has just arrived." He then asked, "It's nice to see you guys again. What would you like: a hot-dog, or a hamburger?"

"Two of Each please, and the same for me lass."

Sylvia pointed to the coffee and said, "Don't be shy and help yourself."

Some ten minutes later, Bruce questioned, "So, what Hollywood studio are you from? And what is it, that you want from us?"

Patrick stared at Bruce, then inquired, "Hollywood? Where is that?"

Bruce leaned over to his wife, and whispered, "Get the butterfly net. We have a couple of live ones." He then stated, "You know, Hollywood, California, where they make the movies. You're dressed up like a leprechaun, and your friend over there is made up like a fairy. Which means your actors now. Right?"

"Who's acting? This is me normal attire."

"Patrick, leprechauns do not have a Scottish accent."

Patrick asked, "Alexis, come here, and show Bruce your wings."

Bruce smiled down at Alexis, as she fluttered her wings saying, "See, they are real."

"Great set of wings, and the way you move them is fantastic. Are you two in special effects?"

Alexis held up her finger, and said, "I thought a Pixie getup would put some spunk in Sylvia. Now if you will excuse me I have to shed my wings."

Patrick finished his meal, and stated, "Don't ask questions just, get in the vehicle, we're going for a ride."

Alexis shouted, "Buckle your seat-belts, and hold onto your hats, because we're outta here!"

Patrick let out a yell, as he floored the gas and tore across the waist land at top speed. Dodging rocks and bushes along the way. When the campground was nowhere to be seen, Patrick stopped the ATV, turned around, and said, "Now we can talk. Did a tall thin man dressed in green spandex visit you two?"

"Why yes. My husband was dying from a knife wound when he walked in and saved his life."

"Do you know if he injected your husband with anything?"

"He had the bedroom door closed, so, no one could see what he was doing."

"Bruce, have you noticed any physical changes since then?"

"I am stronger."

"How strong?"

"I snapped a baseball bat in two without any effort, if that is what you mean by change."

"Hand me that green bag with a white leaf on it will you please?"

Patrick took out a stethoscope, and said, "Bruce, could you take off your shirt, so I can listen to your heart and lungs?" Patrick listened to Bruce's heart and lungs then said ma'am, would you mind, if I checked you too?"

Sylvia leaned forward and allowed Bruce to unzip the back of her dress, and asked, "Okay, now what?"

"Could you lower the front of your dress, lassie, so, I can check your heart? I'll close me eyes."

Patrick closed his eyes and said, "Okay ma'am, tell me when you are ready." Sylvia swallowed, as she slipped her arms out of her dress, and said, "I'm ready."

Patrick asked, "Alexis, place me stethoscope on her chest."

Sylvia grumbled, "Hey Doc, that stethoscope of yours is cold."

When Patrick was finished, he stated, "You can get dressed now. I've heard enough."

Bruce held his wife in his arms and asked, "Well, Doc?"

Patrick looked at Sylvia and said, "You, lassie, have a heart flutter, and will need a pacemaker in three years if it goes unchecked."

"That's right. My doctor told me last year that I was dying but she was wrong."

Patrick squeezed some gel in an inhaler, gave it to Sylvia, and said,

"Breathe deeply until the unit beeps." He turned to Bruce, and said, "Your heart and lungs are strong."

Bruce quickly stated, "You brought us out here just to tell us something we already knew?"

"No. I have a proposition for you. It pays fifteen thousand dollars a month, tax free, plus, all expenses. Because of your strength and ability, my boss wants to know if you will work for him, as a Marshal."

Bruce queried, "If it is for some crime boss, the answer is no."

"It is perfectly legal. I'll give you all the information you need, so, you can check things out for yourself."

"Can I pray about it?"

"I would expect you to. Oh, there is one more thing I want you to do for me. There is a ball and bat in the back seat. Toss me the ball and stand over there. I want you to hit the ball as hard as you can."

Bruce took his stance and swung, the sound from the bat hitting the ball reverberated through the desert. Patrick exclaimed, "Wow! You tore the cow hide right off that ball! I wouldn't be surprised if they find it in the next county! Just for curiosity sake, let me see, if you can break that bat in two"

"Sure, no problem." Bruce held the bat, and snapped it like a twig."

"Perfect. Now, let's get back because I hear a hamburger calling me name."

Bruce asked, "Who was that man in green and what did he inject in me?"

"Duncan is my boss and had the man in green inject you with an experimental drug and I see it worked."

"Duncan used me as a guinea pig!" screamed Bruce.

"You were dying and it saved your live so stop complaining."

Back at the ranch approximately nine-fifty that night, Patrick shook Bruce's hand saying, "I'll be by tomorrow to check on your wife's heart, here is me card, give me a call when you decide." Patrick turned and said, "Let's go, Alexis."

"Wait. I wanna help Sylvia put away the food, first." stated Alexis.

Minutes later, Sylvia stared at the discarded cups, plates, and napkins, then moaned, "The rest can wait until tomorrow, I'm going to bed. Are you coming Sweet?"

"Be there in a minute." Bruce tossed Patrick's business card on the table and retired to the bedroom. In the middle of the night, Sylvia opened her eyes and thought Bruce, was Randy, lying next to her, let out a scream, then began to furiously kick and pound him. Bruce grabbed her arms hollering, "Sylvia, wake up! You're having a nightmare!"

She opened her eyes, saw, Bruce next to her and cried, "I am so sorry Sweet, Did I hurt you? I thought Randy was in bed with me."

"Don't worry, it's just a slight relapse. Let me pray for you."

After the prayer, Sylvia curled up next to her husband, and slept through the night. In the morning, Bruce was up first, and asked, "Sweet. What do you want for breakfast? French toast, pancakes, or waffles?"

Sylvia shouted from the bedroom, "Pancakes with apple slices in them." She walked out of the bedroom clad in white shorts, and a white halter top, sat at the table outside, and took a sip of her tea. Glanced up at her husband staring at her with his eyes and mouth opened. She asked, "Is there something wrong?"

"What are you doing outside in your underwear?"

"I'm wearing a white halter top and shorts. Is there something wrong?"

"Yes. Patrick is going to be here, today to check your heart, so, why don't you put on a dress, or something."

Sylvia smiled sweetly and inquired, "Do you remember what happened last night?"

"Yeah. We met Patrick and Alexis who took us for a wild ride, then checked our vitals."

"I had to sit in the back of that stupid ATV, trying to keep the front of my dress down, while Patrick played Doctor."

"We were in the middle of nowhere, so, no one saw anything except me and Alexis."

"That's not the point. Somebody could have come by and seen us. I don't want to be known as a cheap floozy!"

"Ah, Sweet. I think you are letting your imagination run wild."

Sylvia snickered, "You are right. Sorry. I'm just trying to save face. When Patrick checks my heart and lungs today, this time I won't die from embarrassment."

Bruce questioned, "Why don't you wear something like that around the ranch?"

Sylvia stood up, slowly twirled around saying, "We have twelve men working for us. What do you think would happen if I sauntered in front of them dressed like this?"

"Point, well taken."

"But, for your sake Sweet, I'll wrap a towel around my waist."

Patrick pulled up in his ATV with Alexis, and hollered, "Anyone for a ride in the desert?" Promptly walked up to Sylvia, put his green medical bag down, took out his stethoscope, checked her heart, and said, "One more treatment should do it." He handed her an inhaler and stated, "Same as last night."

Sylvia looked at it, and questioned, "Is there any side-effects from this?"

"Nope, none. What you are inhaling, is a mixture of herbs."

Alexis sat next to Sylvia and commented, "Nice halter top. I see, you are a lot like me. When no one is around. You let it all hang out." Alexis leaned close, and whispered, "Did you ever sneak outside, at night, in your unmentionable, then when you got back inside you prayed that no one saw you?"

Sylvia glanced at Alexis and just, smiled.

Patrick helped himself to a cup of coffee, and questioned, "Have you prayed about my offer?"

"I'm not sure, that I want to be in law enforcement."

"What are you going to do with your new-found talent? Suppress it?"

"Look, I'm happy with the way things are, in my life."

"So, it's a no?"

"That's right. I am not going to run around this country chasing bad guys."

Patrick stared up at Bruce, stuck his finger in his face, and stated, "You have to get beyond what happened to Pete in that tournament. He knew the risks that was involved."

"The answer is still, no."

"Okay, suit yourself. But, if sometime in the future you decide to take Duncan up on his offer. Just give me a call."

CHAPTER 4

YET ALIVE

At the campsite following Patrick's visit, Sylvia wore shorts and a halter top and nagged her husband to teach her how to defend herself. Bruce took a fighting stance, and said, "Okay, let me see if you can do a roundhouse kick to my face. Don't worry, you won't hurt me."

Sylvia jumped up and nailed Bruce sending him on the ground groaning. She then asked, "I'm sorry, Sweet. Are you alright?"

"I will be in a few. By the way, my face is not down there. Next time, aim higher."

"Let me help you up. Then I'll get you something cold to drink." Sylvia sat next to her husband with a cup of hot tea, and inquired, "So, do you think, I am ready?"

"Definitely. Just, keep practicing a couple of times a week so, you don't get hurt."

"Hey! Since tomorrow is our last day camping, what do you say, we go to Red Lobster in Flagstaff and put on the old feedbag."

"Sounds good to me. Are you going to be dressed like that?"

"I could wear my jean shorts, and a halter top tomorrow but that would not be ladylike. You're the only man that I allow to see this much of my body"

A pizza delivery car raced up to the campsite and skidded to a stop. Sylvia quickly covered herself, as the man jumped out, handed Bruce a large sausage and mushroom pizza. Bruce gave the man a hearty tip, and bellowed, "Dinner is served!"

"Why didn't you tell me, you were going to order a pizza!"

"I thought I would surprise you. So, dive in before it gets cold."

Sylvia took a slice, and questioned, "Are you going to take Patrick up, on his offer?"

"No. Chasing bad guys, is not my idea of fun. Besides, I have a ranch to run."

"Fifteen thousand a month, plus, the expense is nothing to sneeze at."

"All that money will only bring sorrow into our lives. Besides I will not put your life in danger."

"News flash, Sweet. I've already been down that road with Randy."

"I still say it's no! End of discussion."

The next evening, Sylvia put on a yellow skirt that went down to her knees, a white button-down blouse, and did her hair the way her husband likes it. Bruce took his wife's arm and said, "Shall we paint the town red?"

Sylvia paused, stepped back and said, "Let me take a look at you hubby of mine. Not bad."

Inside the restaurant, they had just finished their meal when Sylvia stated, "I just remembered, "I left my purse in the SUV, I'll be right back."

When Sylvia reached in the vehicle, to get her pocketbook, she felt a gun in her back, and a voice said, "Don't scream, or try to run. Just, do as I say."

"Randy," grumbled Sylvia, "You know when my husband finds you here, you are going to be singing soprano for the rest of your life." Sylvia spun around to leave stating firmly, "I am not intimidated by you so, but that stupid gun away."

Randy's face turned red with rage as he grabbed her and landed a hard right cross to her jaw knocking her out, put her in his pickup, and took off for the motel several miles away.

At the motel, Randy threw an unconscious Sylvia on the bed when the phone rang. He answered, it saying, "I can't, I'm busy right now. I'll be there in an hour." hung up the phone, went back to the bed, when the phone rang again. The manager hollered over the phone, "This is the front desk. Your credit card is no good. You have to come up with another means of payment, now!"

Randy's heart pounded, as he stared at Sylvia out cold, lying on the bed, he then thought, I'd better take care of things at the motel office first then I can come back and have my fun with Sylvia, as long as I want. Randy took off Sylvia's shoes shoved it under the bed to prevent her from running away, and left the room.

Twenty minutes later, Randy walked out of the office, spotted Sylvia trying to get away in his truck. Sprinted across the parking lot, yanked the door open, shoved her to the other side of the seat, saying, "If that's the way you want it. Fine with me. I know of a place where it will be just the two of us and you can scream all you want."

Sylvia tried to jump out of the truck as Randy slammed his fist into her face throwing, her limp body against the passenger's door.

Randy stepped on the gas and, took off out of the parking lot toward the freeway. Ten miles south on route 60, the sun was setting, as the traffic came to a crawl because of road work. Sylvia opened her eyes, glanced at Randy, saw her chance to get away, and opened the door to jump out. Randy reached over, cough her skirt, and tore it. Sylvia screamed as she jumped out of the pickup, raced to the side of the highway, around the trees and bushes, over the rail-rode tracts, and into the waist-land. Where she tripped over something, fell to the ground, and passed out.

Sylvia woke several hours later, looked at the moon and sobbed, "Lord please help me. I'm lost, afraid, and I hurt from the beating and where the shrubs scratched me."

Twelve minutes later, the wind picked up and Sylvia moaned, "No Please no. I don't need it to rain." Sylvia turned her back to the wind as the rain started to fall. Minutes before the sky opened up a deluge, a large tarp hit her in the back. She turned around, and shouted, "Thank you, Lord! At least I can keep dry." She sat on a boulder with the tarp wrapped around her shivering in the cold wet darkness, grumbling, "Great, here I am in the middle of nowhere, but I am thankful I found my shoes."

The next morning, the hot sun beat down on Sylvia sapping the strength as she trudged through the desert trying to find her way home. At two in the afternoon, Sylvia stopped, looked around at the cactus, sagebrush, and rocks, shook her head and said, "Maybe I should have let him. No, just thinking about it makes my skin crawl. I'm sorry Bruce, I can't make it home." she then, collapsed on the ground.

Hours later, a woman in her mid-fifties clad in jeans stopped her Land-rover, jumped out to check if Sylvia was alive. She grabbed a bottle of water, and revived her, saying, "You're going to be alright." she put Sylvia in the vehicle, and headed for her cabin, not too far away."

Late that evening, Sylvia opened her eyes, and asked, "Where am I?"

"I'm Annie, and you are in my home. Now, tell me. Why were you running around in the hot desert? And what happened to your face? It looks like you ran into someone's fist."

Sylvia whispered, "I was kidnapped by Randy and he tried to beat me into submission. But it was only by the grace of God that I escaped."

"Did you ah, give in to him?"

"No. that's why I am still dressed."

"Is there anything you need?"

"Yes. Call my husband Bruce Jay Birdson his cell phone number is 928-555-1213. And do you have something for my nasty sunburn?"

"Just the other day I fell hair to a whole case of sunburn cream. I'll give you the phone, so you can call your hubby. While I apply the cream."

"Great, you can start from my head and work your way down to my feet."

Sylvia called her husband and sobbed, "Hi Sweet, I'm alright, Randy kidnapped me, but I managed to get away."

"I'm so glad you are safe; I'll be there as soon as I can."

Twenty minutes later, Bruce knocked on Annie's door. She opened it, and said, "Come in out of the heat, I've been waiting for you."

"How's My wife doing?"

"She is sleeping right now, but it's a miracle, that she is yet alive."

"Oh? How So?"

Around three-thirty, in the afternoon I saw the buzzards circling west of here and thought a poor animal had died from the scorching heat and went about my business. But, the thought kept coming to me to go check and see. That's when I found your wife lying face down in the desert sand. She told me that some guy by the name of Randy had kidnapped her and tried to force himself, on her. When she refused, he tried to beat her into submission."

"Did he?"

"No, your wife is a feisty woman and was able to escape."

Bruce opened the bedroom door, crept in, knelt by the bed, and held his wife's hand, and stared at the multiple contusions on her face. Then vowed, "Randy is going down hard, if it's the last thing, I do."

Sylvia opened her eyes, saw Bruce and said, "Hi Sweetheart. I'd give you a hug and kiss, but, I hurt too much."

"That's alright, you get some rest." and left the room.

At the kitchen table with Annie, Bruce called Patrick, and said, "Sylvia needs your help, and I am your man."

"Be there in ten minutes."

Later, Patrick entered the home with Alexis, and inquired, "Where is the lass?"

Annie got up, and said, "I'll show you," and walked down the hall.

Bruce leaned over and quipped, "Alexis Where are your wings?"

"I normally hide them around humans." Then giggled.

Twenty minutes later, Patrick walked into the kitchen five minutes after Annie and said, "I gave your wife something for the pain. Which means, she will be sleeping for a day or two." Patrick handed Bruce a 44 Magnum, and a metal ID card and said, "Here you go, Marshall. If I were you, I'd stop that fellow Randy, once and for all." Patrick stuck his nose in the air, and asked, "Is that scones, I smell?"

"Just baked a fresh batch yesterday. Would you like some?" asked Annie.

"I thought you'd never ask. Oh, did you know, that you have a cream-colored Maine Coon Cat in your bedroom?"

"It finally came out from hiding, I found it a week ago, and the only time it comes out and that is to eat, then it goes back to hiding."

"It has taken a shine to Sylvia; the thing is curled up by her side."

Bruce stated eagerly, "We'll give it a good home."

"Good, you can take the food, toys, and litter I bought for it," stated Annie.

Two days later, Sylvia walked into the kitchen, carrying the cat in her arms, and questioned, "Can we keep him, Sweet?"

Back at their motor home, the cat immediately made a beeline for the bedroom, and curled up on the bed, and went to sleep. Sylvia suggested, "Why don't we call her, Flash."

Bruce took his wife in his arms, and said, "I promise, the next time Randy strikes, I'll be there to put his lights out."

Sylvia inquired, "Do we still have some of that pizza left?"

"How about if I throw a few dogs on the grill?"

That night, they were disturbed from their sleep, by Flash persistent meowing, Sylvia sat up in bed, and hollered, "I smell smoke!"

Bruce opened the bedroom door to a raging inferno, quickly closed the door saying, "Get dressed. We gotta get out of here."

Sylvia opened the door and screamed, "The whole front of the motor home is up in flames, we're trapped!"

"No, we're not." Stand back." Bruce took a deep breath and hammered the back of the home with his fist until he had torn a hole big enough for them to crawl through. Minutes later, the entire camper was in flames.

Sylvia stared at her husband in his PJs bottoms, and giggled, "You look cute like that. But I think, you better put some pants on before the fire department gets here."

After the fire was put out, the Fire Marshall walked up to Bruce and asked, "I'm glad you all are safe. Do you have any idea how the fire started?"

"No. my wife and I don't smoke. My wife and I were asleep and our cat woke us up. That's when we discovered that the camper was on fire."

The police approached Sylvia, put his light in her face, then growled at Bruce, "Would you like to explain how your wife got those bruises on her face?"

Sylvia cuddled close to her husband, and explained, "It so happens I was kidnapped several days ago, and he did this to me when I tried to get away."

"Did you file a complaint against him?"

Bruce showed the officer his ID and said, "I'm a Marshall, and I am handling the case."

The officer took the ID, glared at Bruce, and said, "I'll be right back."

Eight minutes later, the police officer handed the card back saying, "You check out. Sorry for doubting you, Sir."

The fire chief caught Bruce's attention, and reported, "It looks like the work of an arsonist. Someone deliberately built a fire under your camper, for the sole purpose of killing you two."

Silvia held flash in her arms as she sat at the picnic table with her husband and asked, "Have you called Harry to come to pick us up?"

"He should be here in 20 minutes."

CHAPTER

5 DEJA VU

Back at the ranch weeks later, Sylvia rolled over in bed, to discover that her husband wasn't there. She then remembered, "That's right, He had to go to Flagstaff to do some investigation into Randy's background. Flash jumped on the bed brushed against her side purring. Sylvia muttered, "Alright, I'll feed you. Can't a body sleep late for a change?" She walked out into the kitchen, with just, her pink PJ, and fed the cat. Seeing the back door ajar, she closed it, grumbling, "I wish Bruce would learn to close the doors after him." fixed herself a bowl of dry cereal, and walked around munching on her breakfast, and thinking, now, *"This is what I call relaxing. I can let it all hang out, without being seen."*

Standing by the fireplace, she heard a noise coming from the far room, put her bowl on the mantel, picked up the poker, and went to check it out, and found a pair of men›s cowboy boots in the middle of the floor with dirty white socks stuffed in them. She went to pick them up, then thought, no, Bruce is going to have to learn to pick up after himself. She returned to the fireplace to finish eating her breakfast, but, found a man›s shirt on the floor. Angry that Bruce was such a slob, she picked it up, and threw it in the fireplace to burn it, grumbling, "That›s it, he is going to be minus one shirt. That will fix him."

As the shirt caught fire, she heard a noise coming from the bedroom and thought the cat was shut-in. Upon opening the door, she saw a pair of men›s jeans, lying on the floor by the bed, and muttered, "On no. Randy›s in here, turned to go, when two strong arms grabbed her from behind, held her close, and shouted, "Stop struggling! as he kissed her on her neck.

"This can't be happening to me," thought a panic-stricken Sylvia terrified over what was about to take place.

Randy turned Sylvia around, held her by her shoulders, and hollered, "Where is your Bruce now?"

"Don›t do this to me!" screamed Sylvia.

Sylvia kicked him, in the stomach, jumped, and raced into the living room, looking for Bruce›s gun.

Randy walked in the living room, and said, "You have no one to help you, and nowhere to run. You might as well give up because you know I am going to get what I want from you."

Sylvia stared at Randy, and screamed, "I›d rather die than have you touch me!"

"Oh, that can be arranged."

Sylvia spotted a hunting knife on the fireplace mantel, then said, "Alright, you win. I›ll lay down on the bearskin rug for you, but, you will have to get me a pillow from the bed."

As soon as Randy›s back was turned, she grabbed the knife and shoved the knife into his back, Randy turned around, looked at her in shock disbelief, reached his hand out to touch her once more, and fell, dead."

Sylvia dropped the knife, sat by the body sobbing. The next thing she knew she was in bed with Bruce, who was telling her to wake up. She stared at her husband, and said, "Thank you. I had that stupid dream again."

"You mean the dream where you knifed Randy?"

"Yeah, that one."

"Not too ticked off at him are you?"

Sylvia sat on the edge of the bed, put her feet on the floor saying, "Clara won›t be here until ten o›clock. That gives me three hours to relax."

"Aren›t you going to get dressed?"

"Nope. I like walking around with my nightshirt and bottoms until Clara gets here." Sylvia walked out into the living room, spotting a bone-handled hunting knife on the fireplace mantle, and asked, "Sweet. Where did this knife with the initials A.R.K. come from?"

"I found it on the front porch, yesterday morning. None of the ranch hands wants to lay claim to it. So, it looks like it›s mine."

Sylvia fed the cat, fixed herself and her husband a bowl of dry cereal, and a mug of tea, and questioned, "What have you found out about Randy?"

"He›s been arrested eight times for assaulting married women, but none of them would press charges. He was arrested five times for carrying a concealed weapon, and a string of robberies a mile long, but, no one would press charges."

"Do you think he is intimidating the victims?"

"Most likely. But, the trick is to prove it."

Sylvia went into the bedroom to change, saw a small blue blinking light over the window, and hollered, "Bruce, can you come in here for a moment?"

He poked his head in the room, and asked, "What›s up?"

Pointing to the object Sylvia inquired, "What›s that?"

Bruce took it down, looked at it, and said, "It›s a small spy cam." He then asked, "Sweet, you keep your computer running 24/7, don't you?"

"Sure do, Why?"

"Turn it off for a bit. I want to see something."

Sylvia shouted from the den, "It›s off!"

"The webcam just went off too. Do me a favor, keep it off for a few days."

Sylvia walked back into the bedroom, and queried, "But, what about my best friend, Twila? She will think I›ve dropped off the end of the Earth if I don›t email her several times a day."

"Did you e-mail her that we were going camping?"

"Sure did. She wanted me to tell her all about the trip. Why? I even told her about your trip upcoming to Flagstaff."

"Please tell me, no, on this question. Did you text that we were going to the Red Lobster?"

Sylvia hung her head, saying, "Yeah."

"You may not like this but, your best friend Twila, in fact, is Randy."

"But, Twila is so, sweet and kind. It›s impossible that it could be that piece of garbage, Randy."

"Have you seen her in the flesh?"

"No. She lives in Alaska."

"Okay, keep talking to her. but, limit your information until I check her I.P. Address."

"You›ve got it."

"Now, let›s check every nook, and cranny of this house, to see if we can find any more of these spy cams."

Clara walked in, and stated, "It›s gonna be another hot one. What are you two up to?"

Bruce tossed the spy cam to her and said, "We are looking for something like this."

"I saw one the other day, in the den."

"Good, you check there, Sylvia, you take the kitchen and I›ll search the living room. Then we›ll all check the spare bedrooms."

Four hours later, a pile of listening devices and spy cameras was placed on the coffee table in the living room. Sylvia stared at her husband, and stated, "Now, will you do something about Randy, besides research. Or, are you going to wait until he slits my throat?"

"For one, I don›t know his address, and there is no proof, that Randy planted these in the house."

"Are you forgetting what he did to me?"

"No,"

Clara suggested, "I›ll make a pot of coffee, and tea. Then I want to speak to you, Sir."

Ten minutes later Clara handed Bruce his coffee, and Sylvia her tea, and stated. "Bruce. You have to let go of the past before you foul up your future. What if your wife›s reoccurring dream is a warning from the Lord?"

"I doubt it."

"Whether it is or isn›t, you need to act, before it is too late," warned Clara.

"Alright, I›ll do something." Bruce approached Harry, and ordered, "Have Joe, Donny, and Ted guard the house, if they see Randy, shoot him, but, don›t kill him. Harry, Herb, come with me. We need to find Randy›s old haunts."

"He usually hangs out, at the Broken Horn Saloon just outside of town."

Bruce gave his wife a kiss saying, "Sylvia, I promise I won›t get hurt." Bruce picked up his gun and headed for the SUV with two men. On the way there, Herb tapped Bruce›s shoulder, and said, "We can›t take the law into our own hands."

Bruce showed Herb his ID, and stated, "I›m a Marshal, and I want to scare the crap out of him."

Bruce stopped his SUV in front of the saloon, stepped out, and directed, "I don›t have to tell you guys, what to do if things get a little rough." Bruce opened the door, spotted Randy shooting pool, and said, "Randy, I want to talk to you, outside."

Randy straightened up, leaned on his cue stick, and said, "Hey, guys, this is the piece of work that has that great looking Babe for a wife, I was telling you about." Eight burly men stood in front of Randy with their arms folded across their chests.

"Three to one!" shouted Harry, "Who wants a fat lip first?"

Bruce picked up a cue stick, and said, "Gentleman, let›s not be hasty."

"Let›s not." shouted one man as he charged Bruce only to be sent flying backward into his buddies. Another thug attacked and got a roundhouse kick to his face. "Seconds later, a free for all broke out, while Randy crept out the back door. Bruce spotted him, picked up the 8 balls, and threw it at Randy, sending him flying to the floor. Grabbed him by the back of his collar, and said, "Surprised to see me? Probably not. After all, you're the one that bugged my home, so you could spy on Sylvia."

"Didn›t I hear on the news several weeks ago, that your wife was lost in the desert?"

"Strange, my wife survived, and is talking up a storm, naming you, as her kidnapper. Oh, just to inform you, your spy cams are permanently offline. Or, should I call you, Twila?"

Randy kicked Bruce in the stomach, and sprinted away, Harry walked up, pivoted his Winchester up, and fired, sending Randy to the ground. Bruce asked, "You didn›t kill him, did you?"

"Nope, I just shot him in the leg."

Standing over Randy, Harry stuck his rifle in his face, and said, "Make one move and I›ll blow a hole in you wide enough for a semi."

"You›re not going to get away with this!" screamed Randy, "I›ll sue you, for everything, you have."

Harry growled, "Shut up." and struck him in the head, knocking him out.

Herb approached, and questioned, "What do we do about his buds?"

Harry quickly spun around, fired a shot in the air, saying, "Gentlemen. Think about it."

Three patrol cars screeched to a halt, the policemen jumped out and leveled their guns at Bruce, and Harry shouting, "Put your hands up."

Bruce stated, "I›m Marshal Birdson and the man on the ground, is under arrest for; kidnapping, assault, arson, and attempted murder." he showed them his ID and shoved Randy in the back of a cruiser.

On the way back to the ranch, Herb showed Bruce a stack of receipts, and said, "I found these in Randy›s pickup. There are three from an electronics store for surveillance equipment, a receipt from a gas station on the date, your wife was kidnapped."

"Looks like I have to go to Flagstaff tomorrow, and check this out. You two want to come along?"

Early the next morning, Sylvia rolled over in bed, and noticed, that her husband had left for Flagstaff already. Flash jumped on the bed brushed against her side purring. Sylvia grumbled, "Alright already, I›ll feed you. Can›t a body sleep late for a change?" She walked out into the kitchen in her bathrobe and fed the cat. Noticing the back door was slightly open, she closed it, muttered, "I wish Bruce would close the doors after him." then muttered, "Deja vu. This was in my dream."

She shrugged it off, fixed herself a bowl of dry cereal, and walked around, munching her breakfast, and thinking, *"Now, this is what I call relaxing. I can let it all hang out, without being seen."*

Standing by the fireplace eating her breakfast, she heard a sound from the far room, put her bowl on the mantel, picked up the poker, and thought, this is too weird, I›d better get dressed, and see if I can get hold of one of the men. Outside, she caught Stud›s attention, and said, "I think someone is in the house."

He took his rifle, carefully opened the door, to find a man›s shirt lying on the living room floor. Sylvia whispered, "That›s not Bruce›s, he always picks up after himself. Check the bedroom, but, be careful."

Stubs pushed the bedroom door open with his gun, to find no one. Randy came up behind Sylvia, stuck the hunting knife to her throat, and demanded, "Drop the gun, or Cutie here, gets it."

Stubs put down his gun saying, "You›re a dead man, Randy."

"I don›t think so. Her idiot husband tried to put me in jail last night, and you see what happened."

Randy backed across the living room towards the front door holding the knife to Sylvia›s throat. Stubs eyes fell upon Flash, slowly making her way around the room, to where Randy was. Then let go a cry, as she sprang on Randy›s back-scratching and biting at him. Sylvia broke free, raced across the room, with Randy screaming as the cat›s lighten fast claws sunk deep into his flesh. Randy charged out of the house, as the cat made one final leap on his back and bit his neck. Flash stood on the edge of the porch with her ears down, growling, watching Randy drive away.

Sylvia sat on the porch step, picked up Flash, and said, "You may not be a good mouser. But, you are my Little Protester."

Stubs shook his head in disbelief and remarked, "I always thought cats were a ball of lazy fur, that slept all day and eat. But I was wrong.

CHAPTER 6

DEATH'S COLD HAND

The next morning, Sylvia was up at the crack of dawn, strutted around the house in her usual skimpy attire. Then cooked a ham and cheese omelet with toast and coffee for the both of them, then went in the bedroom to wake Bruce. He pulled her down on the bed, held her in his arms, and kissed her. Sylvia giggled, "Great idea, but, we don't have time for this right now, our breakfast is getting cold."

After breakfast, Sylvia put the dishes in the sink, crept up behind her husband, and threw her arms around him, saying, "Now, we have time."

Bruce turned around, held his wife in his arms and kissed her, just as someone knocked on the front door. Sylvia›s eyes suddenly widened, as she muttered, "Oh crap. Not now." ran into the bedroom saying, "Bruce answer the door, while I throw some clothes on."

Bruce opened the door and greeted a casually dressed man in his forties. He introduced himself, "Hi. I›m Pastor Giles. Am I troubling you at this hour of the morning?"

"No, no. come on in. Would you like some coffee?"

"You›re a man after my own heart. A little cream, no sugar, if you please."

Bruce sliced some bagels, opened the cream cheese then served the Pastor.

Sylvia walked out of the bedroom, clad in a pale green dress, and greeted the visitor. The pastor stood up, shook her hand saying, "I'm Pastor Giles, please to meet you."

"Have a seat," stated Sylvia when Bruce excused himself to dress.

Sylvia inquired, "What›s on your mind Pastor?"

"I›m not sure. All I know is, the Lord Jesus told me that I was to be here this morning."

Bruce walked out of the bedroom, approached his wife, and said, "I have to check the wind turbines in the west field today, so, I have to excuse myself."

Sylvia pleaded, "Why don›t you tell Harry that you›ll be there later."

Bruce picked up his business cell phone, and said, "Harry. Why don›t you have the guys, take a break? I have a guest and I'll be there later."

Pastor Giles, looked at Sylvia and said, "I am blessed just, meeting you."

"Thank you, Pastor. But, I haven›t done anything special."

Pastor Giles took a swallow of his coffee, and explained, "You›ve been kidnapped, lost in the desert in the scorching hot sun, assaulted several times, and you are still smiling."

Suddenly an explosion shook the house, Bruce rushed to the door to see billows of smoke rising from the west field. The pastor inquired, "Is there anything I can do?"

"No. thank you, Pastor Giles. If it wasn›t for your visit, my men and, I would have been killed in that explosion."

Bruce hollered to Harry, as he ran towards him, "Take the men, and assess the damage! I›ll try and meet you there, later!"

Pastor Giles shook Bruce›s hand and said, "I must be going, Mrs. McNeil wants me to pick up a few things for her. Oh, Sylvia, can you make it to the Bible Study tonight? I want you to shear your testimony."

Bruce stared at his wife and asked, "Are you alright? You looked nervous when the Pastor was here."

"That›s because I have no undies on."

"Excuse me?"

"I didn›t want to keep the Pastor waiting so, I grabbed the first dress I could find, slipped in on without putting anything on underneath, see."

Bruce stared at his lovely wife and said, "I see you›re a bit kittenish today. I still have time why don›t we relax in the bedroom for a bit."

Sylvia dropped her dress saying, "That›s just what I had in mind."

They had only taken three steps when Clara barged in, bellowing, "Lord! It›s a great day, to be outside!"

"Not, from where I›m standing," grumbled Sylvia. She turned and suggested, "Clara. Before you start cleaning the living room. Why don›t you put a load of wash in, first?" Hoping to get rid of her maid, for a while.

"I will, after you two go outside, so, I can do my work. Bruce, your men are probably looking for you. Sylvia, sit somewhere, and enjoy the beautiful weather and relax for a couple of hours."

Sylvia went to go to the bedroom, but Clara quickly ushered her, and her husband outside."

On the front porch, Sylvia kissed Bruce and said, "I›ll be sitting in the gazebo, missing you."

"Don›t you mean the picnic shelter."

"No. I mean the gazebo. You know that cuddly place out back where we can sit and talk?"

"Sorry, Sweet. Because we have so many people working for us. I built a picnic shelter, instead."

"I understand. Now, you can build us a gazebo in the back of the house, just, for us."

Sylvia paused at the edge of the picnic shelter, studied the barbecue pit, picked up a piece of charcoal, sat down on the wooden bench and let go a squeal, and muttered, "Stupid bench just bit my behind." and began to doodle on a scrap piece of wood, mumbling to herself, "Clara is right, I do need to get out more."

Sid happened by a few minutes later, saw what she drew and said, "Stay there. I›ll be right back. Five minutes later, Sid dropped a drawing pad, and pencils on the table in front of her, and said, "Here. You can use this more than I can."

Sylvia looked up at him, and questioned, "Are you sure?"

He sat across the table from her, placed his hand on top of hers, and stated, "I can›t draw a straight line if my life depended on it. By the looks of that sketch you drew, you›re good."

"It›s something I›ve done all my life, and never gave it a second thought that it was good. Thank you, Sid. Hey, you better get back to work before, my husband thinks you're goofing off."

Hours later during lunch. Bruce sat next to his wife and inquired, «Are you alright? You look like you have ants in your pants.»

With a forlorn expression on her face, Sylvia asked, «Can we go back to the house during lunch? Clara will be gone.»

«Sorry, Sweet, the boys want to treat us to lunch. It›s their way of saying thank you."

Sylvia huffed, «Alright. But, I have to talk to you when we get back to the house.»

«Can›t we talk about it here?»

«No.» growled Sylvia.

«Are you sure, you are alright? You look uneasy about something."

«Yes, I›m fine. But bring on the burgers.»

At five o'clock that day, Bruce kissed Sylvia, saying, "The work is finished, the men have all gone home. I am all yours."

"*Yes!*" thought Sylvia walking back to the house with her husband, smiling. Clara greeted them at the door, and said, "Now, didn't that feel good to get outside and get the stink blown off you."

Sylvia cringed, smiled politely, and stated, "Clara. Thank you for your concern. However, Me Boss, you worker. You are a great friend and all that. But, during the eight hours, you are working for me. You don›t tell me, and my husband what to do. Once, you remember that we will get along just fine."

"I›m so sorry I overstepped my bounds, Sylvia. It won›t happen again." Clara talked for forty-five minutes about her son-in-law, and how he is such a wonderful husband, to her daughter. After Clara had left, Sylvia locked the door, and growled, "I thought that woman would never shut up."

Bruce held his wife in his arms, and asked, "Do you want, to tell me why you have been acting like you have ants in your pants?"

"Hello, husband of mine. I don›t have any undies on, and when I sat on that stupid picnic bench, in that shelter of yours, it bit my bottom."

"Come, again?"

"I have a splinter in my bottom! alright!"

"Why didn›t you say something to me, earlier?"

"Yeah, like I was going to announce it to all the men that my butt hurts."

"Sorry, lay down on the bed so I can take a look at it."

Bruce sat on the bed with his wife laying on her stomach and said, "Hold still this won›t hurt, much. Hey, did I ever tell you that you have a cute tushy."

"No, just get that splinter out of it." Sylvia let go of a yell, and said, "Easy, with that needle. Will ya!" She turned over, and said, "I›ve been wanting you all day."

Bruce glanced at the clock on the dresser, and said, "Sorry, Sweet. We have just enough time to grab a bite to eat, and get to the Bible Study tonight."

Sylvia clenched her fists, and screamed, "No, no, no, no, It›s not fair!"

"It›s just that we promised the pastor that we would be there tonight."

"I know It›s just downright frustrating. Every time I think we are going to have some personal time together; something comes in the way."

"Maybe we can get together tonight when we get back from church." Stated Bruce.

"That›ll work for me. Let me take a shower and get dressed. You can fix us something to eat in the meantime."

"Don›t forget to put on some underwear this time."

"Cute, cute.»

Bruce announced, "Dinner is now being served in the dining room! Sylvia entered the dining room clad in a cobalt blue dress that went down to her knees, and commented, "Soup and sandwiches good choice."

"Did you remember to put on your unmentionables, this time?" quipped Bruce.

"Sure did," answered Sylvia as she lifted the front of her dress to prove it to her husband.

"I didn›t know you had powder blue cotton undies."

"Now you know, if we keep this up, we won›t be going anywhere."

Bruce snickered, "It›s hard to believe, my Miss Prim and Proper wife went commando today."

"Don›t you even think of breathing a word about it, to anyone."

Upon entering the church, they sat five rows back on the right. Sylvia fell back in her seat with tears streaming down her cheeks, and whispered to her husband, "No matter what happens, everything will be alright."

After the service, a short man wrapped his arms around Sylvia, and gave her a long hug and kiss saying, "Welcome."

Bruce caught the man›s attention and said, "Hi. I›m her husband. The one with the black belt in Martial arts."

The man quickly let go of Sylvia, and smiled sheepishly.

Pastor Giles approached Bruce and Sylvia, and stated, "We have coffee and pastry downstairs in the fellowship hall, care to join us?"

Bruce pointed to the man that just hugged his wife, and said, "Some people are too friendly, with the ladies."

"I am sorry about that. He is not a member of our church and has been warned about being too friendly with the sisters several times. I›ll have some of my ushers escort him out. But, right now, let›s inflect our flesh with some sweets stuff."

Sylvia woke late the next morning with a note on her husband›s pillow that read, sorry to put you off again but I have a lead given me where Randy is hiding. So, my men and I are going after him and drag him to justice. Five minutes later, the phone rang. Sylvia answered, "Morning. How can I help you?"

Clara answered, "Sylvia. I can›t make it to work today because my car is on the fritz."

"Hey, no problem. Take as long as you need." Sylvia hung up the phone, turned the radio on to an all Christian music station, and relaxed on the bed for a nap. Partway through her nap, the radio went silent, seconds later, Randy grabbed Sylvia by her hair, and dragged her out of bed with her screaming, "Leave me alone!"

Randy stared at Sylvia and screamed, "All I wanted was to have some fun with you. But, no, you had to play hardball." and threw her against the Bureau. Sylvia struggled to cry out, but, couldn›t because of the pain in her side. Randy reached down, pulled her up by the hair of her head, stuck his face in hers, and screamed, "You are not worth the trouble, you've been giving me!" dragged her outside, and threw her down on the front porch, took out his semi-automatic, from his belt, fired a several rounds at her, and stated, "Let's see if you can outrun a bullet."

Sylvia lay on the porch sobbing from the pain, as Randy kicked her in the side hollering, "Get up, you worthless piece of garbage!"

With tears streaming down her face, Sylvia summoned up all her strength, took hold of a wooden chair, to help her stand on her feet, knowing that any minute she was going to see her Saviour. Randy placed his gun under her chin, and said, "Good." Pointing to the dirt road, and said, "Run."

Sylvia didn›t care as her anger burned within her, and, thought, *"If he kills me so be it,"* turned, kneaded Randy, sending him down on his knees, yanked the gun out of his hand and ordered, "Get up!"

Randy slowly stood to his feet, and quickly landed an uppercut to Sylvia›s jaw, sending her tumbling backward over the porch railing. She jumped to her feet and sprinted to the barn in terror with bullets dancing around her feet.

Sylvia crouched down in the horse stall, held her breath as she watched Randy slowly walk by saying, "You know you can't hide from me."

After Randy had passed the stall, Sylvia carefully climbed on top of the gate and leaped on Randy›s back sending the gun flying, with her landing in a pile of hay. He scrambled for the gun, picked it up, kicked Sylvia, in the side, then placed his foot on her stomach, pointed the gun at her head, and said, "Goodbye."

A bullet knocked the gun from Randy›s hand, as Bruce screamed, "You touch my wife again, and I›ll kill you, where you stand!"

Randy slowly raised his hands, asked, "You won›t shoot an unarmed man, will you?"

As soon as Bruce lowered his gun a little, Randy pulled a handgun from the inside of his shirt and fired. Sylvia grabbed the fallen gun ready to kill Randy, but before she could, he jumped on one of the horses and escaped.

Bruce hollered, "Let him go! We›ll get him later." he knelt by his wife, and inquired, "You, okay?"

"I am now."

Bruce quickly, held her in his arms, comforting her, as the men closed the barn doors, to give Bruce some privacy with his wife.

Sylvia looked up at her husband, and asked, "Aren›t you going to go after Randy?"

"We now, have the time, and the place to enjoy each other."

"But the men will know what we are doing."

"So, what you are saying is you want to wait until later, am I right?"

"I didn›t say that."

CHAPTER 7

A BREATHER

The next morning, Sylvia rose around ten, took off her red nylon nightshirt, put on a yellow dress, and asked, "Sweet when are you going to get up this morning?"

"I'm gonna sleep in today. Harry and some of the men went to do some snooping around, to see if they can find out where Randy is hiding." By the way, how are you doing?"

"A little sore, but, otherwise I'm doing good. Oh, I put some makeup on to cover up my bruises."

"I thought you told me, that you were so furious, at what Randy did, that you didn't have time, to feel, humiliated when he pulled you off the bed."

"I was embarrassed about what we did in the barn yesterday."

"What did we do in the barn, that made you feel uncomfortable? All I did was be a husband to you."

"Do I have to spell it out for you?"

"No. I'm just giving you a hard time Sweet. Hey. We were alone and had the time, and I did not want to say no to you, again, especially when you looked so beautiful lying in the hay."

"You left out quirky in that list."

"Trust me. The men did not know, what we got into in the barn."

"Be that as it may, we are not going to be doing it in the barn, regularly."

"Admit it, it was fun."

"No comment," stated Sylvia trying to hide her smile.

"Isn't Clara supposed to be here, by now?"

"She called yesterday and said that her car required repair. Now, if you will excuse me, I'm going to make breakfast. What would you like? Eggs, cold cereal,

"How about, Eggs, bacon, English muffin, and you."

"Sorry, I'm not on the menu this morning." Just then, a knock came to the door, Sylvia opened it and said, "What's wrong Mack? you know where the propane tank is."

The look on the propane delivery man's face told Sylvia that something was deadly wrong. As he ordered, "Get your husband, cat and get out of the house."

"What's wrong?"

"I'm not sure, but I think there is a bomb attached to your Propane tank."

Sylvia yelled, "Bruce, get Flash, we have to leave because there is a bomb attached to our propane tank!"

Two hundred yards away from the house, Bruce, dressed in his Pjs bottoms held his wife waiting for the news. Forty-five minutes later, a police officer approached Bruce, and reported, "It's a good thing you were late cooking breakfast. Because there was enough C-4 under your tank, to level your house, and barn."

"What does making breakfast have to do with a bomb?" inquired Bruce.

"The detonator was hooked up to a flow sensor. So, as soon as, you turned on your stove, the censor would have detected gas movement, and triggered the explosion."

"Officer, could you do my wife and me a big favor, and check the rest of the buildings for bombs? Because this is not the first time we've had this kind of a problem."

"You have someone trying to kill you two?"

"Yeah, Randy."

"Randy?" questioned the officer? Could you mean Artie Randal Kaufman? His fathers is Judge Kaufman."

"That explains, a lot."

"By that, you mean every time Randal is arrested he's walked you are so, right."

The police officer stared at Sylvia, for a few seconds, then said, "You're the woman, who was lost in the desert."

"Sylvia smiled, and said, "Yes, Randy was the reason why I was there, and I don't want to get into that, thank you."

"I understand. If you ask me. I think someone should shoot him, instead of arresting him. It would make this place safer, for a lot of women."

Some two hours later, the police officer reported, "The dog couldn't find a thing. Oh, is that your 44 Magnum in a case, in the house?"

"Yes it is officer."

"Can I see the permit?"

"Sure, can." Bruce walked into the house, showed the officer his metal ID. The officer contacted the police station, then, five minutes later he handed the card back saying, "Sorry Sir. I had to check things out."

The officer took a picture out of his shirt pocket, and, said, "Could you keep an eye out for this woman. She's wanted by the police for bomb-making, robbery and attempted murder."

Sylvia gasped, "Good Lord! That's Clare, our maid!"

"That explains the C-4. It's a miracle, that you two were not murdered in your sleep by that woman."

Bruce asked, "Can I have this picture?"

The officer leaned close to Bruce, and stated softly, "If you want to go after Randy, his father has a cabin a mile or so off, Poudre Canyon, Highway, in Livermore, Colorado. You can bet his girlfriend, Clara will be there, too. Oh, if something happens to Randy that you can't bring him back alive, there won't be a tear shed. Because, my partner's daughter was molested, by that creep."

"Understood."

After the bomb squad left, Sylvia questioned, "Bruce, how about a bowl of cold cereal, for lunch?"

"Since it's that late, how about, you make your famous Ranch sandwiches while I take a shower?"

"Do you want me to wash your back?"

Late that afternoon, while Sylvia was resting, Harry walked on the porch, sat next to Bruce, and said, "Well Boss, Randy is not in the state, that is for sure. I have evidence to believe he may have gone to Colorado."

"Good, tomorrow, we go to Randy's place to check things out."

"But, Boss. Don't we need a search warrant?"

Bruce held up his ID. and said, "This is all the search warrant I need. As for probable cause. The attempted murder, and assault on my wife, is all I need."

Harry walked in the house, poured himself a cup of coffee, came back out, sat on the porch railing, and asked, "Anything happen while we were gone, Boss?"

"The house, Sylvia and I were almost blown up that's all."

"Randy, maybe?"

"No. Hold on to your mustache, for this one. Our housemaid, Clara, is Randy's girlfriend, and set enough C-4, to level, this ranch."

"You mean that kind, gentle is in cahoots, with that Weasel?"

"Yup. But, I keep getting the feeling, that there is a large piece missing to this puzzle."

"Like what, Boss?"

"Where did a couple of lowlifes get the dough to buy; C-4, computer, and surveillance equipment with? And I know, he did not buy, that semi-automatic weapon over the counter."

"Oh, how is the misses doing?"

"She is fine, on the outside. But, she seems too stressed out, if you ask me."

"Tell her that the boys are pulling for her."

"I will. Tomorrow morning, have Studs send two men in ATVs to check out the fence line. Wind turbine 55, is a little sluggish. The rest of the men are on guard duty except, you and Herb. You two, with me."

After Harry left, Bruce crept in the bedroom, sat on the edge of the bed, and leaned over to kiss his wife. She woke suddenly screaming and hitting him. He grabbed her arms shouting, "Sylvia! It's me!"

Sylvia fell into Bruce's arms crying, "I am so sorry. I thought I was being attacked again."

"I think I need to call Patrick. Maybe he can prescribe something for you."

"Fine. As long as I'm not in the middle of the desert when he uses that ice cube he calls a stethoscope on me." Sylvia gave her husband a kiss and said, "Could you put some lotion on me before I make supper?"

"No problem."

Sylvia rose to her feet, stripped down to her underclothes, looked at herself in the full-length mirror and was horrified over the pealing sunburn, and moaned, "Look at me. I resemble an alligator the way my skin is pealing. especially my back."

"From where I am standing you look great Sweet." Stated Bruce.

"Just hurry and put the lotion on me, so, I can cover up my hideous looking body." Sylvia leaned forward while Bruce applied the lotion to her, suggesting, "Have you ever thought of starting a group?"

"Oh, no. I am not going to get into any of those twelve-step programs when the Lord Jesus Christ provided everything for me through the finished work on the Cross."

"Then, that's, what you should do. Start a group that encourages Christians to look forward to the Cross for their need, and to stop focusing on their failures."

"It's hard to have faith when you're always stumbling over the same weakness."

Bruce turned his wife around and said, "So, stop complaining over the fact that your sunburn is pealing."

"You're right, it's who's I am, that counts."

Sylvia slipped on a polyester nightshirt, and stated, "We have leftovers for tonight."

That evening, as the sun was setting, Sylvia made herself a mug of herbal tea, walked out on the porch, and sat in the chair, deep in thought. Bruce stood in the doorway, drinking his coffee, staring at his scantily clad wife, wondering what was bothering her. He sat in a white Adirondack chair on her left, took her hand, and asked, "What's on your mind?"

Sylvia looked at her husband, with tears in her eyes, and stated, "It just, came to me. It is only by the Grace of God that I wasn't killed when I ran to the barn trying to get away from Randy. I could hear him shouting at me, and the sand hitting my legs when the bullets hit the ground, but, I wasn't hurt."

"Do you mind, if I ask you, what happened after you were kidnapped?"

After Randy struck me, I don't remember anything until I came to lying on the motel bed. All I thought, of was getting out of there, and ran to the truck to escape, only to be hit by him, again. The next thing I remember is the pickup slowing down, I opened the door, to jump out. Randy grabbed me by my skirt and ripped it. I wiggled out of his grasp and escaped."

"Can I ask you this? Did Randy ever you know?"

"No, that never happened, and Lord, I am so, thankful for that. Because, if he did. It would have been more than I could have handled and would have driven me loony, for the rest of my life. Now, can we put this behind us, and concentrate on kicking Randy's butt?"

Sylvia cuddled close to her husband and said, "Let's just sit here, and watch the sunset."

"Aren't you concerned that someone will see you dressed in a short nightshirt?"

"No. We are the only two people on an eight-hundred-acre ranch. Who is going to see me in my nightshirt, but, you?"

"Good point. But I never knew you liked," Sylvia interrupted Bruce and said, "There is no one around, so shush up, so we can enjoy the moment."

CHAPTER 8 TURN AROUND

The next morning, Sylvia rolled over in bed, placed her head on his chest, and asked, "What would you like to do today?" Upon hearing a car door slam, she picked up her head, and said, "Dang. Company. I'll get it." and raced to the door, with Bruce hollering, "Put some clothes on for Pete's sake!"

Sylvia poked her head around the open door, and greeted, "Patrick, Alexis, nice to see you guys. My husband and I are just getting up, why don't you give us a few minutes, to get dressed." Sylvia closed the door, and hollered, "Change of plans Sweet, get dressed, we have company!" Sylvia dashed into the bedroom, threw on a dress with a paisley design, that went down to her knees, rushed out into the living room, to greet her company.

Patrick calmly stated, "It is time for your complete physical. Alexis is a PA now, and will assist you in the unit, outside."

Sylvia moaned to herself, *"What am I going to do? I've gone commando again, and I don't want Alexis to find out."*

Bruce entered the living room and suggested, "Why don't we all sit down, for breakfast, first?"

Sylvia kissed her husband on the cheek and whispered, "Thanks for coming to my rescue."

After breakfast, Alexis took Sylvia for her exam, Bruce stared at Patrick, and said, "Thanks for coming, but, you didn't come all this way just to check out my wife. What's up?"

"The boss wants you to be more aggressive in your pursuit of Randy. Because, if you don't, the big boss will getaway leaving you with a lot of explaining to do to Duncan. That's if, you are still alive."

"I'm not sure that I can kill someone."

"Then he will definitely kill you, and I don't have to tell you what will happen to Sylvia."

"But, if I kill Randy, I will be arrested for murder."

"If you don't, Randy will make a short work of you and your wife. So, what is it going to be?"

"Then it's either do or die. But, why the pep talk? I planned to go after Randy today. Which should close the case."

"Ah, no. You have to look at the whole picture. Not just, one corner of it."

Alexis walked in, showed Patrick the results of the exam, and questioned, "What do you think?"

"Her stress level is red line, that's for sure."

"What about if we give her some medication to bring it down?" stated Patrick

"Good Idea," stated, Alexis, "But in this case, we need to find the cause, before we dish out medicine."

Sylvia growled, "She has a name."

Patrick looked up at Sylvia, and said, "You have got to relax. Your blood pressure is way too high."

"How can I? When I'm scared out on my mind, that Randy will come back, and kill me."

Patrick showed Bruce, Sylvia's medical chart, and said, "See how high your wife's BP is? That means, if you want to have your wife around next year, you have to take out Randy."

Alexis whispered something in Patrick's ear, then muttered, "I see. Check it out." Patrick looked up at Bruce, and asked, "What happened during that kickboxing tournament with Pete?"

Bruce sat down, so, he could look the leprechaun in the face, and said, "We were pretty well matched, Pete; won one, and I won one, and the last match would decide who was going to win the title. I was taking quite a pounding, in the last match. I mustered all my strength and landed a roundhouse kick to his face, sending Pete down on his back. But, this time, he never got up. The Medea dubbed me a killer of someone, with a wife and three children. From that time on, I vowed not to fight again, because, I did not want to be known as a murderer. I know, I should bring down Randy, but I keep seeing Pete's face in my mind."

Alexis handed Patrick the information, he requested, and stated, "Bruce, you didn't kill Pete. He died of an Aneurysm, during the match."

"Are you sure? It was all over the news, and in the papers that I killed Pete. There wasn't a word said about his Aneurysm."

"Here, read it for yourself."

After reading Pete's medical report, Bruce sat down, and said, "This says that Pete had the aneurysm long before he stepped in the ring. If that is true, then his wife should never have collected on his life insurance policy." Bruce put his head in his hands and cried for five minutes. Picked up his head, and said, "Thank you, Patrick. You lifted a ton of weight off my shoulders. Then a smile formed on Bruce's face, as he stated, "Randy, your days are numbered."

Patrick shook Bruce's hand saying, "It's time, we got moving along. See you in a couple."

After Patrick left, Bruce looked at the clock and said, "Sylvia. We have just, enough time to pack and take a shower. Which will be mine."

Sylvia growled, "No you don't, that shower is mine, you pack."

"I haven't had a shower in days." snapped Bruce.

Sylvia inquired, "How big is the shower?"

"About eight-foot square. Why"

"You start the water, and I'll join you in a minute."

"Sounds good to me. Just remember, we shower, then we get out and dress. No horsing around."

Sylvia replied with a devilish smile, "It never entered my mind."

Forty-five minutes later, Sylvia walked out of the shower, grabbed her towel, tossed Bruce, his, and asked, "Who was the one that said no fooling around?"

"When it comes to you, I have no willpower."

"That makes the two of us. Oh, are we going to Randy's place first, so we can find clues as to why he is so obsessive over me?"

"Yes, that and Clara's place too."

Harry knocked on the door, and hollered, "Are you ready to go? It's getting late."

Sylvia answered the door saying, "Dressed, packed, and ready to go."

Harry studied the smile on Sylvia's face, and said, "When you two lovebirds are finished doing whatever, let me know. I'm gonna make myself a cup of coffee and sit on the porch."

Later, Bruce pulled his blue SUV in the driveway of a small ranch home. Got out, and stated, "Harry, you go around to the back, and in one minute you bust in. I'll take the front and do the same. Sylvia, you stay in the vehicle."

"Not on your life."

Inside Randy's home, Harry remarked, the place has been stripped clean. I have to hand it to this guy, he's smart."

Sylvia slowly walked from room to room, and stated, "Clara was living with Randy. This place is too clean for a man."

Harry left to check the trash, came back two minutes later, handed Bruce Randy's old phone bill pointed to a name and stated, "That's Mr. Tucker, CEO of the large land development company that been hanging around Wickenburg, here of late. My guess is, Tucker hired Randy to chase you off your land."

Sylvia walked up to her husband twirling a pair of women's red bikini undies on her index finger, and said, "I guarantee you, that these do not belong to Randy."

Bruce stared at Harry and asked, "Why didn't you tell me Clara, was your sister?"

"That's because she's not."

A heavy-set man barged in brandishing a rifle, and hollered, "Freeze!"

Harry smiled and stated, "You don't want to do that."

"What are you doing in my friend Randy and his wife's house?"

Harry grabbed the gun barrel, jerked it out of the man's hands and said, "You're so-called friend, is wanted for attempted murder, arson, assault, and a few other charges that have slipped my mind. Tell me. Have you ever seen Randy hanging around a man, called Mr. Tucker?"

"Sure have. I've seen them in town talking just the other day. The man turned his head, saw Sylvia, and stated, "You're the woman that was running around the desert."

Sylvia cringed, and replied, "For your information, I was trying to escape from your good friend Randy, who had kidnapped me."

Harry tossed the gun back to the guy, and said, "Next time, choose your friends wisely."

Bruce glanced at Harry, and stated, "Looks like a dead end. We might as well close this case, who knows where Randy is by now."

"Inside the SUV, Harry remarked, "Good thinking. If he is close friends to Randy, you can count on it that he's gonna tell Randy that we are clueless."

"Colorado, here we come." stated Bruce.

Halfway to their destination, Bruce stopped at a quaint little inn on route 14 in Colorado. Sylvia whispered, "Sweet, where is the lady's room?"

Bruce pointed at the two rows of blue and white shanties, and said, "Pick one."

"They're porta potty's!" grumbled Sylvia, "I wouldn't be caught dead, in one of those disgusting things."

"Sorry, the only thing left is the tree across the street."

"You're impossible!" screamed Sylvia, as she stormed off to the portable outhouse.

Harry chuckled, "I take it your wife isn't used to the great outdoors."

"But she sure has a lot of moxie," stated Bruce.

Hours later, at a food and fuel in Livermore, Colorado, Bruce, stated, "This is not what I expected. Where's the motel?"

Harry took out his cell phoned and said, "I've got you covered." called a friend and said, "This is Harry, and it's payback time. I'm here in Livermore, with my friend and his wife and we need a place to stay. I'm sorry about your dinner getting cold, but, how about the next time you're in a fix, I don't show up." Harry ended his conversation, smiled, and said, "There is a family up the road, that will put us up for a week if necessary."

A short time later, Harry knocked on the door of a light-yellow house, a man in his fifties answered the door, asked, "What can I do for you, mister?"

Sylvia hollered, "Uncle Leo!"

"Sylvia?" I haven't seen you in ages. What are you doing, this far west? Come in come in, I'll get my wife."

Leo glanced at Harry, and said, "Your friend, Harry, just called, and yes, you can stay."

Bruce extended his hand saying "I'm her husband, and would you know of a man by the name of Kaufman? He is supposed to own a cabin around here."

"Sure do. His son and his wife live in it now." Leo stared at Bruce, and said, "You're here to arrest him aren't you."

"I guess his reputation proceeds him."

"Forget about Randy for now, because we were about to sit down to dinner."

"I'm sorry uncle that we came at the wrong time."

"Nonsense, there is plenty to go around. So, sit and eat. Then we talk."

Sylvia tapped her aunt's shoulder, and asked, "Please tell me, you have an inside bathroom."

"It's down the hall, on your right."

"Yes!" shouted Sylvia in relief.

After a hearty dinner, Sylvia retired to her bed, for the night. The next thing she knew, Randy was there with her. All Sylvia did was closed her eyes, and whimpered, "No. This can't be happening to me!"

Bruce woke his wife, saying, "You've had another nightmare."

"Yeah. Tell me about it," grumbled Sylvia.

"Is it the same dream about Randy?"

"Yes. Can you hold me?"

When Sylvia saw the first rays of the sun shining through the window. She rose, dressed, and went into the kitchen looking for a cup of tea. Her aunt approached her, and said, "From the moment you walked in, I knew something was wrong."

Sylvia poured herself a cup of tea, and said, "I've been attacked by Randy several times, but, fortunately, I am still alive to talk about it."

"However, you are scared that one day, Randy will assault you. Don't receive that lie from the Devil."

"I may sound redundant, but, can you please pray for me?"

"Sure, but, you must accept the fact, that Randy did attack you, and the Lord will not put more upon you than you can handle."

"Thanks. It's finally sinking in."

"Don't worry, you will get through this. Just keep your eyes on the Cross, and what He did for you."

CHAPTER 9 TURNABOUT IS FAIR PLAY

After a hearty dinner, Sylvia retired to her bed for the night. The next thing she knew, Randy was on top of her, she screamed, "Get off me, get off me!"

Bruce woke her, saying, "You've had another nightmare."

Seeing the first rays of the sun shining through the Window, Sylvia got up, dressed and went into the kitchen looking for a cup of tea. Sylvia's Aunt Lea approached her, and said, "From the moment you walked in, I knew something was wrong."

Sylvia poured herself a cup of tea and said, "I've been attacked by Randy several times but fortunately nothing ever happened."

Sylvia's aunt quickly stated," You're scared that it will finally happen. Don't receive, that lie from the devil."

"I may sound a bit, redundant, but, can you please pray for me?"

"Sure, but, you must accept the fact, that it did happen to you, and the Lord will not put more upon you than you can stand."

"Thank you. It's finally sinking in."

After breakfast, Bruce picked up his gun, and said, "It's time to arrest Randy."

Leo suggested, "We'll take my pickup. Your SUV will stick out, like a sore thumb. Prayerfully I can distract him."

Later at Randy's place, Leo turned off the engine, and let his truck roll to a stop, got out and said, "You two wait here. "Let's see, if we can catch Randy off guard." Leo glanced towards the truck and knocked on the door. Clara answered and asked, "What can I do for you, Leo?" she glanced suspiciously at his truck, then back in the house and said, "Randy isn't here."

The garage door suddenly exploded, as Randy backed his truck through it hollering, "Let's go!"

Clare shoved Leo off the front steps, jumped over the railing and made a dash for the truck.

Harry jumped out of the truck, leveled his Winchester at Clara, and fired, sending her sprawling, on the ground.

Randy stepped on the gas, sending dirt flying, as he sped across the lawn trying to make his getaway.

Leo shouted, "Take my truck and go after him! I'll stay here until help arrives."

Harry hollered, "Bruce, I'll drive, you do the shooting."

The tires squealed, sending up smoke, as Harry and Bruce took off after Randy. Upon catching up to Randy on the highway, Bruce leaned out the window, and fired, knocking out the back window."

Randy tried to return fire, as he flew down the highway at top speed.

Harry suggested, "Bruce. See if you can take out his rear tire."

"I can't, from here."

"I'll pull alongside him. Then see if you can get him to stop."

Harry floored the gas and was almost even with Randy, Bruce stuck his rifle out the window and ordered, "Give yourself up, before It's too late!"

Randy swerved his truck into Harry, trying to knock them off the road. Bruce fell back in the cab, hit Harry's arm sending the truck fishtailing back and forth across the road.

Harry slammed on the breaks, regained control of the truck and stated, "When we catch up with him pump the cab full of lead. One of them has to hit him."

As they were about to, catch up to Randy, he slammed on the brakes, drove the truck in the ditch, grabbed his rifle, and headed for the trees. Harry brought the truck to a skidding stop, Bruce jumped out of the truck and fired at Randy hitting him in the leg.

With Randy cornered behind a tree, Bruce hollered, "Randy, I'm a Marshall, and you need to give yourself up! You have nowhere to run!"

Randy fired four shots nicking Bruce's shoulder. Harry suggested, "It's either he dies, or we do. I'd much rather die in my rocking-chair, then by a bullet. So, here's what we'll do. When I go to my left, Randy is going to poke his head out, to shoot at me. That's when you take him out."

Harry glanced at Bruce, leaped out in the open, rolling on the ground trying to dodge the bullets while Bruce took careful aim, and fired. Randy's gun went silent. Harry sighed, in relief. I think we got him."

"Just to be on the safe side, be ready, just in case he is playing possum."

Bruce stared down at Randy, and said, "Yup. He's dead. I haven't seen anyone live, after being shot between the eyes."

Harry commented, "Not bad, for a Greenhorn."

Bruce glanced over his shoulder and said, "It looks like we have attracted a little attention, from the police. Shall we put our hands up."

Surrounded by a dozen state police, Bruce stated, "I am Marshall Birdson, and this is my deputy. I am going to reach in my pocket for my ID."

The officer looked down at the dead body, and said, "Mr. Kaufman finally met his match." he checked Bruce's ID, and said, "We'll take it from here."

"We had to take out his live-in wife Clare who is back at the house."

"She was taken to the hospital with a bullet to the chest, but, she will live to stand trial." The officer looked at Bruce's shoulder and asked, "Do you want someone to look at that?"

"Thanks, but, no thanks. It's just a scratch."

Harry suggested, "Shall we go back to Randy's place and snoop around?"

Bruce parked the pickup in the driveway, got out, as Leo questioned, "Did you get him?"

"Yes, Randy will not be bothering anyone anymore. Now, let's look for clues."

Leo stared at Bruce and said, "That shoulder of yours needs looking after.

"It'll be alright. He just winged me."

Finding no clues, they returned to Leo's home. As soon as Sylvia saw Bruce's shoulder, she let go a squeal saying, "You told me that you would be careful!"

"It's not much of a wound."

"Not much" screamed Sylvia, your whole shoulder is full of blood."

Lea, asked Leo, "Get me the first aid kit from the bathroom. Bruce take off your shirt, and let's see, what you've done to yourself." Lea turned to Sylvia, and said, "Hold up your husband's arm while I clean him up."

"You look like you've done this before."

"You know it. I'm used to patching up Leo, every time he decides to start a project."

"I'm always careful, "stated Leo.

"What about the time you, decided to fix the lawnmower and sliced your arm."

"It was just a scratch."

"I don't call an eight-inch gash, a scratch."

Bandaged up, Sylvia hugged her husband, and said, "Can I see you in the bedroom for a minute?" Sylvia closed the door, put her head on Bruce's chest saying, "Thank you. Sweet. I am so glad Randy is dead. Now I can feel safe again."

With his arms around his wife, Bruce replied, "Shooting someone in the head isn't something I like doing, but, it was either him or us."

Sylvia sat on the bed, kicked off her shoes, patted the mattress with her hand saying, "All I want right now is to snuggle with you."

Bruce joined his wife on the bed, took her in his arms, and fell asleep. A knock came to the bedroom door and Lea, stated, "Supper time, you two."

Sylvia opened her eyes, and said, "Lord, I feel great. Come on Sweet Cheeks, time to put on the old food bag." Halfway out the door, she stopped, turned, and saw her husband struggling to put on his shirt. She smiles and said, "There are times to be indecent, and there are times to call for help. This is the time to say something."

"I can manage." insisted Bruce.

Sylvia tenderly kissed him on the cheek, and stated, "No, you can't, and for the next eight weeks or so I will be by your side to help you."

"I said, I can manage."

"Bruce H. Davidson. You have given me more than I ever hoped for. At least, let me do something, to show you how much I love you by, helping you, in your time of need."

"I guess, I have been kinda hard-headed."

Sylvia assisted Bruce, to put his shirt on, saying, "It's a wife's job to fuss over her man. Now, hold still so, I can tuck your shirt in."

"Take it easy with my left shoulder."

Sylvia poked her head out of the room, and wondered, where is everyone? She then hollered, "Lea! Leo! Hello!"

"In the basement," shouted Leo. "Come on down and join the fun!"

In the basement, Bruce commented, "Nice rec room, Leo."

Sylvia caught her aunt's attention and inquired, "Why all the people?"

To welcome your husband in the family, and to pray for the Lord Jesus's protection over him."

Leo bellowed, over the din of the crowd, "Alright, everyone! Gather round Bruce, and pray as you feel lead."

Ten minutes later, Bruce found a seat to enjoy a mug of coffee and finger-food. Harry sat next to him, leaned over, and stated, "Of course you know judge Hoffman is going to be pounding on the door first thing in the morning wanting your hide for killing his son."

"I'll be ready for him."

"If he starts anything, "I'll have him in my sights in seconds." stated Harry.

Seven o'clock the next morning, Judge Kaufman pounded on the front door screaming, "Bruce Birdson I want to speak to you, now!"

Bruce slipped on his pants, opened the front door, and said, "What's the matter with you judge? Don't you have enough respect, not to bother people at this hour of the morning?"

The judge pushed his way inside, screaming, "You killed my son in cold blood! For that, I am going to see that you die for your crime!"

"Keep your voice down people are still sleeping."

"I could care less! I'm going to see to it, that you pay for killing my innocent son!"

Harry leveled his rifle at the judge, and ordered, "Settle down Judge, or I'll put you down."

"You can't threaten me! I'm an officer of the court of Arizona!"

"You also forced your way into this home. Which is breaking and entering. So, judge, if you don't want me to drop you where you stand, go back out that door and ask to come in so we can talk." Harry fires a shot and bellowed, "The next one counts, Judge!"

Judge Kaufman stormed off, threatening, "I'll be back with a warrant to arrest both of you."

Bruce stated, "Harry. Shooting at a judge is not healthy even if he is in the wrong."

Harry unloaded his gun, and said, "How can they arrest me for shooting blanks? All I did was, scare the pants off a bag of wind."

Bruce chuckled, "Yeah, he probably has to go back to the motel and change his undies."

Sylvia came out of her room and asked, "Whoa! Who cut the cheese?"

"That would be Judge Kaufman, and he went home to change."

Lea approached and said, "Now that the whole household is awake, I'll start the coffee, and breakfast, Sylvia, why don't you set the table."

Three hours later, a knock came to the door, Lea opened it, Judge pushed his way in the house with two police officers, pointed to Bruce and ordered, "Arrest him for the murder of my son, Randal Kaufman."

The officer quoted Bruce his right as he put the handcuffs on him.

Bruce stated, "I am Marshall Birdsong, and I shot Randy for assault, attempted murder, resisting an arrest, just to name a few."

"I don't care, who you are. You murdered my son and now you will pay."

A well-built, six-foot-tall, man, in his early thirty's clad in a dark grey suit, walked in, took off his sunglasses and said calmly, "Take off those handcuffs."

The judge hollered, "He is being arrested, for the murder of my son."

"Marshall Bruce Birdsong was arresting Randy because of the mile-long priors. Now, take off the handcuffs."

"I don't care who you are Sir, I can have, you arrested for obstructing justice. So, back away so, the officers can do their duty."

The stranger snapped his fingers, and two men clad in dark gray suits brandishing automatic weapons swiftly stepped out of the back of a black Mercedes, rushed to the door. The man handed the officer a letter and stated, "I'm Duncan, and this will explain everything."

The police officer handed the letter to the judge, saying, "Sorry Sir, this guy is legit. This letter nullifies the arrest warrant and puts you under arrest."

The two men in gray suits pointed their weapons at Judge Kaufman, and Duncan stated, "You, judge Randall Kaufman, the First, is about to undergo a life-altering trip, One, which you will never return from." Duncan gave Bruce a hug, saying, "Good job, But, it is not over yet. He turned to Sylvia, took her hand, bowed, and kissed it saying, "Your beauty and grace exceeds the women of the ages." He then left.

Sylvia giggled, "Oooo. That guy just gave me goose pimples."

CHAPTER 10 A TRAIL OF BLOOD

They arrived back home two weeks later, Bruce ripped the condemned notice off the front door grumbling, "What do they mean condemned?" and went to enter, when Sid, rushed up, saying, "Hi, Mr. Birdson. Sir, you can't go in there."

"Why not? It's my home."

"The building inspector was out here last week because someone had filed a complaint, so he labeled all the buildings, structurally unsound."

"He can't do that. These buildings were already approved. There has to be a mistake."

"There is no mistake, Sir."

Harry, remarked, "Mr. Tucker is an octopus with his tentacles into everything. I wouldn't be surprised if the building inspector is on his payroll."

"What do you suggest, I do?"

"I'd call in an inspector that won't be persuaded, by Tucker's money."

"You can't do that." snapped Sid.

Okay, then, I'll call the inspector back, and have him explain to me what is wrong."

Sid brushed against Sylvia's chest, as he left. She turned and glared at him and brushed it off as an accident. Then followed her husband into the house.

Harry inquired, "Do you want me to hang around?"

"I wish you would, I was about to call the building inspector. But first, we have to pray and give this into the hands of Christ, and seek His direction."

Later, Sylvia made a pot of coffee, and the three of them sat on the front porch, in the wooden Adirondack chairs talking, and enjoying their coffee, waiting for the inspector. Forty-five minutes later, a red Chevy SUV skidded to a stop, and a thin man dressed in a white shirt, and jeans hopped out of the car shouting, "You're not supposed to be in that house!"

Harry reached down, placed his hand on his Winchester, as Bruce stated, "When I built this ranch, you inspected all the buildings, then, you told me that they exceeded the building codes. Now, you're telling me that they are unsafe. Who's paying you to write a false report?"

Harry shot the front tire, on the inspector's car, and said, "You are not going anywhere until you come clean."

"You can't kill me in cold blood."

"I don't intend to," replied Harry, "I'm just going to make your life real uncomfortable. Now, start talking."

"If I tell you, he'll kill me."

"If you don't, I will show your boss, the fabricated lie you concocted, so, Mr. Tucker can get my land. "stated Bruce. He leaned forward, and asked, "How much is he paying you?"

"Two hundred thousand dollars, because, he wants to sell the land to a developer for top dollar."

Bruce walked up to the inspector, and ordered, "You will remove all the building violations from my property. If you don't, I will make sure that you don't have a job tomorrow."

With the buildings approved again, Harry stated, "I'll remove the rest of the signs, and call the men back to work, tomorrow."

Inside, Sylvia picked up Flash, in her arms, and questioned, "If all the men were laid off by the inspector, what was Sid doing hanging around."

"I have no idea."

"I'm going to grab another mug of coffee, and sit do some sketching, at the picnic shelter."

"I'm gonna get some much-needed sleep." stated Bruce.

Sylvia sat at a table under the picnic shelter and began to sketch a desert scene. Sid sat close beside her, and inquired, "Where is that wasteland scene?"

"One from where I was lost."

Sid put his hand on top of Sylvia's, and asked, "Ever thought about taking a romantic walk in the desert when the sun is setting?"

Sylvia removed her hand from Sid's, and answered, "Nope."

"You are missing out on something fantastic."

"Sid, you are a nice guy, and all but if you will excuse me I want to finish this drawing."

Sid placed his hand on the lower part of her back and watched Sylvia draw. She promptly stopped, and growled, "Sid, please take your hand off my thigh."

"I am sorry, I did not realize what I was doing. I'll see you later."

"Not, if I can help it," muttered Sylvia.

The next day, Duncan approached Bruce and inquired, "Somebody is killing young women and I want you on the case."

"No thank you, Sir." Bruce strapped on his 45 Magnum, kissed his wife saying, "Pretty Nightshirt, it doesn't cover much, But, I like it. Oh, Harry and I are going to pay Mr. Tucker a visit."

In Mr. Tucker's building in town, Bruce pushed his way past the guards, up to the receptionist, showed her his ID, and questioned, "Where is Mr. Tucker?"

"He is in a meeting."

Harry pointed to the hand-carved mahogany double doors on their right, and said, "He's probably in there."

Bruce kicked the doors in, and bellowed, as he approached the conference table, "Mr. Tucker, Sir. I hear you want my land and are trying to force me off it by using a squeeze play."

Two security guards rushed in, Harry spun around, leveled his Winchester at them, and ordered, "Lose the guns. We're here for a friendly chat. So, let's not turn this into a shooting match."

Mr. Tucker calmly replied, "I have no idea, what you are talking about. Even if I was trying to force you off that worthless piece of land you call a ranch you would have to prove it."

"Oh, that's easily done, and when I do. You, Sir, will be finished in this town."

Mr. Tucker slowly slid his hand under the table, Harry leveled his Winchester at him, and said, "Keep those hands where I can see them, or the word 'the late.' will be added to your name."

Bruce smiled, and stated, "Oh, your building inspector. He just cleared my ranch of all its violations." turned, and left.

Noticing that the secretary wasn't at her desk, and Tucker's office door was open Bruce whisper, "Harry stand watch while I check his office."

Bruce entered Tucker's office, found a photo of Sylvia on his desk with an X mark on her and a memo to the Building inspector to condemn Bruce's ranch, and would pay him two hundred thousand dollars after the job was done. Bruce pocketed the information and left.

Outside, Bruce watched helplessly as the flame engulfed his SUV, took his car key, tossed it in the fire, turned to Harry and stated, "It is times like these that I would feel justified, in blowing away that piece of work, Tucker."

"Don't let him push you into doing something stupid, Boss. Then, he'll win."

"Let's go for a cup of coffee."

"You can use my truck until you get a new SUV. Don't worry about me, I'll sleep in the bunkhouse."

At a local coffee shop nearby, Bruce showed Harry what he found, and asked, "What do you think?"

"I think Tucker is trying to defeat you, through your wife."

"You mean, 'divide and conquer?'" questioned Bruce.

"Yes. If Tucker can get one of his cronies to seduce Sylvia, the ranch will be his, and you know he's already tried to do that, and failed miserably."

"Then, it's time we got going because I need to buy a new vehicle."

Bruce drove home, late that afternoon with a pre-owned burgundy Ford SUV. Sylvia dashed out of the house, saying, "I like the color but, why did you buy it? The old one worked just fine."

"Someone set it on fire, outside Mr. Tucker's office."

Sid walked up, stood next to Sylvia, brushed his hand on her thigh, and started smiling, "Spending the wealth, I see."

Sylvia moved to the other side of her husband and remained silent. Sid meandered close to Sylvia brushing her thigh. Sylvia grabbed his hand and screamed, "Keep your hands to yourself!"

Bruce grabbed Sid and was ready to rearrange his face when Sid pleaded, "I am sorry. I didn't mean, to touch your wife there. It won't happen again."

Bruce let Sid go, saying, "Okay, this time. But, I don't want to see you around my wife again."

As Sid scurried away, Harry stated, "I'll send him to the dentist to have his teeth put back in if you want."

That evening after supper, Sylvia sat in one of the rustic-looking wooden chairs, showed Bruce the gazebo she wanted him to build, and said, "I want it two hundred yards from the house, with a flagstone walkway to it, white gravel around it with shrubs."

"I think I can manage that."

Harry walked on the porch, sat next to Bruce, said, "Evening Mrs., Birdsong."

"Can the formality Harry, it's Sylvia."

Harry reached over, took the pad, and asked, "Did you do this?"

"Just my doodling, no biggy."

"You're good. He turned the page, looked at Sylvia, then, at the drawing, and said, "That's you, sitting on the rock, with your head in your hands."

"Yeah, that's me, lost in the desert."

The inspector skidded his car to a stop in front of the house, jumped out hollering, "You've got to help me. Tucker is trying to kill me!"

"Are you sure?" inquired Bruce.

A black car stopped some ways off, a shot was fired, and the inspector's lifeless body fell to the ground."

Harry stood to his feet, looked down at the inspector's body, and commented, "Yup, he's sure."

Patrick parked his car by the side of the house, walked up to Bruce, with Alexis, and asked, "Do you know that you have a dead body lying on the ground?"

"Yeah. The poor guy ate some of Sylvia's cooking." quipped Bruce.

"Sylvia belted Bruce in the arm, saying, "That's not true."

"What's the reason you're here?"

"Can't I just pay you a friendly visit?"

"Sure, but, that friendly visit always announces bad tidings."

Harry gave Alexis a hug, saying, "You've got to be the prettiest woman there is."

Alexis's face turned red, as she giggled, Sylvia rose to her feet, gave her husband a kiss, and said, "I'm going to tend to the horses. I'll see you later."

Sid followed Sylvia into the barn, and commented, from a distance, "Do you know you have nice legs."

"Sid. My husband told you to stay away from me."

Sid moved a little closer, and remarked, "It's hard not to touch you when you have such a great body."

"One step closer Sid, and I'm calling my husband."

Sid grabbed Sylvia from behind, put his hand over her mouth saying, "All I want to do, is talk." Sylvia tried to wiggle free. Sid took a knife from his pocket, stuck it under her chin and said, "You scream or try to run, I'll knife you. Now, we are going to go to the barn doors, and close them."

With the barn doors closed, Sid tied Sylvia's hands together with a rope, threw it over the rafters, and hoisted her up until she was a foot off the floor. He then stated, "This is what you are going to do. You are going to convince your husband, to sell the ranch to Mr. Tucker."

"And if I don't do as you say?" growled Sylvia.

Sid put a gag in her mouth, picked up a horsewhip, cracked it close to her face several times saying, "You will convince Bruce." the next whip crack caught Sylvia's side ripping her blouse. She shook her head in defiance.

An infuriating Sid screamed, "You will do as I say!" and furiously beat her back with the whip.

When Sid was finished, he yanked the gag out of her mouth, stuck the point of his knife to her chest, and warned, "If you tell your husband that it was me, you will get more of the same. Now, what are you going to do?"

Sylvia let out a long shriek, sending Sid into a panic, shoved the knife in Sylvia just as Bruce, Harry, Rick, and Alexis ran to her aid. Sid dashed out the back of the barn and hightailed it into the desert in hoped to escape.

Bruce grabbed his wife as Harry lowered her down, and asked, "Who did this to you?"

"I recognize that knife, it's Sid's," stated Harry.

Patrick fought back his tears, as he stated, "She'll be alright. You go after Sid."

CHAPTER

11 DEAD MEN TELL NO TALES

After an hour of chasing Sid in the desert on horseback, and not finding him, Bruce suggested, "We might as well give it up, Harry. It will be dark soon."

"I've got an idea. Sid is a kinda fella that will camp somewhere until morning. So, let's wait until dark maybe we can spot the glow of his campfire."

"Sounds like a perfect idea."

As the last glimmer of light was fading, Harry slowly scanned the desert, pointed to his left, and said, "If that does not look like a campfire, I don't know what does."

Bruce checked his 44 Magnum, to make sure, it was ready, Harry suggested, "Let's have some fun with him before we beat the crap out of him for information."

"I'm game. Let's go."

The two casually rode into Sid's campsite, tied their horses to a bush. Bruce stated, "Don't get up on our occasion, we saw your campfire and thought we'd have a friendly chat."

Harry picked up a metal dinner plate, and said, "Bruce, look he has made a pot of coffee, beans and hot dogs with a side dish of potato salad. I think Sid wants us to help ourselves. Harry smiled at Sid, and asked, "You don't mind, do you?"

Sid remained silent staring at the campfire. Bruce questioned, "You ah, expecting somebody? I notice that you have two-bed rolls and there is only one of you."

"It looks like he planned to kidnap your wife, Bruce, to force you into selling your property, to Tucker. But something went wrong."

Sid went to stand, Harry pointed his Winchester at him and stated,

"Why don't you sit down for a spell and tell us all about why you almost killed Sylvia?"

Sid remained silent and stared at the flames. Harry fired three rounds at Sid, and hollered, "I asked you a question, boy. Who paid you to do it? Or, do you just like beating up women?"

Bruce poured a cup of hot coffee, dragged Sid to his feet and threatened as he took a sip of his coffee, "Tell me who is paying you, and who is Tucker going to sell my land to?"

Bruce threw the coffee in Sid's face, took his gun and said, "You were a big man when you tried to beat my wife into submission. Here's your big chance, let's see what you can do, about beating the snot out of me."

Sid stood silently still eyeing Bruce, as he hit Sid several times around the face. Harry stood up, and said, "That's not how you do it. Here, let me show you, and cold-cocked Sid, and said, "That's the way you do it."

"I'll get the rope and tie him up. You check his pockets."

Harry opened Sid's wallet, and said, "Well looky here. A note from Mr. Tucker, it says, Sid, do whatever it takes to force Sylvia to convince her husband into selling the property to me. Don't worry if she dies, I'll cover for you, and what do we have here? A check for fifty thousand dollars that's signed A. A. Tucker."

The next morning, Harry fried up a mess of ham, and eggs for the two of them. With Sid complaining, "Hey that's my food!"

Bruce stuck his gun in his face threatening, "You're lucky to be alive. We have enough evidence to nail your hide to the barn door, so shut up."

Bruce tied a rope to Sid's waist and made him walk behind the horse all the way back to the ranch in the scorching heat. As they were tying up the horses, a single shot was heard, when Bruce turned around, Sid lay dead, with a bullet to the chest."

Bruce asked Harry, "Why don't you get Herb, to help you with the body. I'm going to see how my wife is doing."

Bruce entered the bedroom and saw a woman dressed in white, tending to his wife. He asked, "Ah, Doc. How is my wife doing?"

"HI. I'm Doctor Kimberly Chase. Your wife is doing fine but she needs lots of rest."

"I take it, you know Patrick and Alexis."

"They work for me."

"I have another body, outside. Would you mind checking him out and give your final word."

Kimberly knelt down by Sid's body in the barn, opened his shirt, to check his vitals, when a Western Diamondback Rattlesnake, sprang out from under Sid's shirt and bit her. She let out a scream and recoiled in fear. Bruce shot the snake, picked up Kimberly, and rushed her back inside. The doctor directed I have a snake bite kit in my green medical bag, get it and I'll tell you what to do. Then call Patrick and tell him that I need him here to take over for me."

Bruce treated Kimberly and suggested, "I have a guest room where you can lie down."

"That will be good, thank you."

Harry knocked on the bedroom door and hollered, "You in there Bruce?"

"What's up?"

"All the men have packed up and left expect Herb, Stubs and me. It seems that they don't like all the excitement that's been going on around here of lately."

"Would you want to chat over a cup of coffee? My treat."

Outside, sitting on the porch, Harry questioned, "Do you think, you can keep the ranch going, with three men?"

"I make four. And yes, I know I can. To give up now would be admitting defeat, to Tucker."

"That's what I like to hear."

Harry looked up, saw a silver limo approaching and asked, "I wonder who's the fella in the fancy car is?"

The limo stopped in front of the house the chauffeur opened the back door and A. A. Tucker stepped out dressed in a blue pinstriped suit; walked up to Bruce and said, "I have heard that you have been having all kinds of trouble ever since you bought this miserable piece of land. How's your wife doing? Has she recovered from that nasty beating? I tell you what. To show you that I am a good guy. I'll buy this worthless piece of ground for twice what you, paid for it."

"How did you know that my wife was whipped?"

"I had hired Sid to talk to you nicely about selling me the land but he went and beat her, which was something I did not tell him to do. So, I am firing him as of today."

"You're a little late for that. Someone put a bullet in him this morning."

Mr. Tucker wrote a check for a tidy sum, handed it to Bruce, and said, "Here is something for you to think about." Bruce ripped up the check, put it in Tucker's suit pocket saying. "Keep your blood money. I am not selling my ranch. Good-day, Sir!"

Mr. Tucker calmly walked past Bruce, and in the house to go into the bedroom, where Sylvia was. Patrick stood in the bedroom doorway, with his arms folded across his chest, and said, "Don't even think of coming in here, Tucker."

"All I want to do is to see how Sylvia is doing."

"I'm her doctor, and I say, you are not allowed in."

Harry shoved his Winchester in Tucker's back saying, "I'm the security around here, and you take one more step, I'll pull the trigger. Now, what's it going to be?"

Bruce grabbed Tucker by the back of his collar, and his belt, picked him up and threw him through the screen door onto the porch. Harry poked his Winchester rifle out the door, and stated, "You step one foot on this property again and there won't be, a Mr. Tucker."

Mr. Tucker asked, "Harry. How is your wife doing? Oh, that's right she died leaving you alone to deal with a lot of hurt and pain and is the reason why you are not thinking right and became a slave to Bruce, I tell you what, I will give you fifty thousand dollars to work for me."

The chauffeur quickly pulled a gun from the inside of his coat. But before he could use it, a bullet from Harry's gun stung his hand. Mr. Tucker, stated, "If that's the way you want to play it fine with me. I can oblige Bruce in a fight but, when the dust settles, I will have the ranch and Bruce will have nothing. Think about my offer. Good-day."

Bruce walked up to Harry, watched Mr. Tucker drive away, and asked, "How are the wind turbines doing?"

"Turbine 75 is a bit sluggish, but on the whole, I would say, things are going well. How's the missus doing?"

"The doctor gave her a sedative so, she could get some rest, and Patrick sent Kimberly home to take care of that snake bite. How are the men doing?"

"Stubs and Herb have left for the day, and I am gonna stretch out for a while. I'll see you later.

Patrick caught Bruce's attention, and asked, "Can you please give me a hand with your wife? I need to change her dressings." in the bedroom, Patrick stated, "I've already changed the bandage on her knife wound, now I have to change the dressing on her back."

After carefully rolling Sylvia over, Bruce pulled up her nightshirt, and watched Patrick slowly peel off a large bandage from her back, then ask, "How is that possible that the marks on her back are almost gone?"

Patrick grinned sheepishly and said, "It's a new medical breakthrough. Could you hand me the sterilize wipes so I can clean her back?"

"Do you mind if I do it Doc?"

"Sure, go ahead. I'm going to get a cup of coffee and relax."

Alexis entered the room, and asked, "Have you seen Patrick?"

"He's around here nursing his coffee."

"Thanks. I see Sylvia's back has healed nicely. Do you want me to help you change her nightshirt?"

"No thanks. But can you assist me in turning her over?"

Once on her back, Sylvia opened her eyes smiled, and said, "Hi Sweetheart."

"Welcome back to the Land of the Living. How are you feeling?"

"Weak and sore, but, good."

Alexis handed Sylvia something for her pain, and inquired, "Do you want to get up for a while?"

"Could you please get me my long pink bathrobe? I would like to sit on the front porch for a while."

The evening breezes were blowing when Bruce aided his wife on the front porch and set her down, then fixed her a cup of hot tea. Sat next to her and asked, "Are you sure, you are feeling okay?"

"Just, peachy keen, and hunky-dory."

"Come on Sylvia, you are talking to me, your husband."

Sylvia stared at her husband, and said, "Don't even think of giving this ranch up. We moved out here to fulfill our dream, and no pencil-pushing bully is going to take it away from us."

"I was thinking about giving in to Tucker. Because, I am tired of the fighting, I am tired of you being constantly assaulted by Tucker's lowlifes."

"The way I feel, if Mr. Tucker were to walk on this porch right now, I would kick his sorry butt all the way back to the main road."

"Thank you, Sweet."

Patrick came out of the house, placed a TV tray in front of each of them, Alexis, served Chicken Cordon Bleu and said, "Eat up. Your drinks are coming right up. For dessert, there is a slice of deep-dish apple pie and ice-cream."

"Why the royal treatment?" questioned Bruce.

"After what you have been through. You need some relaxation. Now, to add the final touch, Maestro, if you please."

Patrick walked back out on the porch with a gypsy violin. Sylvia giggled, "That is so cute. A leprechaun Gipsy, and I suppose you are going to dance for us, Alexis."

"Give me a minute to change, and your evening will be complete."

After the dinner and music, Bruce looked up and remarked, "It's time to go in, by the looks of those black clouds gathering, we are about to get hit with some horrendous thunderstorms."

"I don't know about you but I love to watch the lightning and listen to the thunder as it rolls across the sky," stated Sylvia.

"Okay, I'll join you. But if it gets too fierce I'm going in."

"Chicken," muttered Sylvia.

A few minutes later, the wind blew the dust around, the sky opened up and a deluge of rain fell as lightning danced around. Bruce helped Sylvia to her feet, as they dashed inside."

Sylvia sat by a window and watched the storm raging outside when Harry banged on the door. Bruce let him in, and asked, "What's wrong?"

"The barn's on fire."

"Are the horses out?"

"Yes."

"The only thing, we can do now is to let it burn then call Ace Lumber tomorrow morning."

Sylvia kissed Bruce on the lips, and said, "I'll see you in a bit, Sweet. I am going back to bed."

Bruce addressed Patrick, and Alexis, "There is a spear bedroom at the end of the hall. "You're welcome to stay until the storm passes. Oh, congratulations on your marriage to Alexis and what happened to Jade after you got her out of prison?"

"She is hiding around Arizona somewhere. Talk to you later, and I am not a leprechaun. I just look like one."

Harry sat by the window so he could see the barn and said, "If you don't mind Sir. I'm gonna sit here and keep an eye on the barn."

CHAPTER 12 CHAMELEON

Nine o'clock the next morning, Bruce stared at the charred remains, of what once was his barn, dreading the cleanup. Harry walked up, placed his hand on Bruce's left, shoulder and stated, "You know what we can do. Is build a wood house? We have enough lumber left over, from the picnic shelter. Then, we can cut and store the burnt wood from the barn in there, and use it for the fireplace, or, the barbecue."

"Great, get Stubs, and Herb, on it right away. I'll call Ace Lumber."

Harry kicked a partly burnt board, uncovering a melted five-gallon, gas can pick it up, and said, "I'll give you three guesses who this belongs to, and the first two don't count."

Just then, they herd Sylvia screaming at the top of her voice for someone to leave. Harry stated, "Looks like Tucker needs another lesson in manners. Do you mind if I have the honor this time?" Harry walked up behind Tucker, while he was trying to convince Sylvia to take the check and asked, "Do you know what the word NO means?"

Mr. Tucker turned around and said, with a smile. "Oh, hey. You're looking good today Harry I only came here to see how you people weathered the storm last night and I was saddened to see that the barn burnt down. So, I offered my assistance by building a new one."

Harry took the check, balled it up it stuffed in Tucker's mouth and said, "One of your goons left this when he burnt down the barn." then, shoved the melted gas can at Tucker.

Tucker, spit out the check, dropped the gas can, regained his composure, and stated, "All I want to do is lend a hand. What's so wrong with that?"

"When it comes from you there is always a catch to it."

"Look, I tell you what I will do I'll buy the lumber for the barn then have my men build it. No strings attached."

Harry smiled, then stated, "You are one sly devil, Tucker, you know that you had your men burn down the barn in a thunderstorm, then you come out here acting all nice, and kind, offering to help us in our time of need. Knowing full well that we would turn you down. Then, you'll call the lumber company, and threaten the owner not to sell us, and wood. I have news for you we will get the lumber we need if we have it shipped from Washington state and there is nothing you can do about it."

"You have me all wrong," stated Tucker in mock innocence.

"Am I?" questioned Tucker.

Sylvia approached Mr. Tucker, and stated through clenched teeth, "You lying snake in the grass. You just threatened to kill me, if I didn't convince my husband to sell you the land."

"The woman is losing it!" screamed Tucker.

Harry escorted Mr. Tucker outside, slammed him against his limo, as the chauffeur tried to intervene. Bruce landed a right cross, to the chauffeur's face, then stuffed him in the front seat, headfirst. Harry pushed Tucker to Bruce, who pushed him in the back. Saying, "You come around here, bothering my wife again and it will be your last!"

"I'll have this ranch yet, Mr. Birdson! Do you hear me?"

Harry spotted a harmless snake, making its way around the edge of the porch, gently picked it up and, said, "Tucker, here is someone that's just your speed." tossed the snake in the back, slammed the door, and ordered the driver to go.

Patrick approached Bruce removed a small micro recorder, from a nearby location and said, "It is all here on tape, Sir. Oh, by the way, Duncan wants to know if you would be interested in taking on the murdered case?"

"I am not into solving murders."

Three weeks later, Bruce was up and dressed, Sylvia kissed her saying, "The lumber for the barn is going to be here sometime this morning. I will most likely see you at lunchtime. Oh, I picked up a stack of Christian magazines for you to read."

Sylvia relaxed in her usual manner, made herself a cup of tea, noticed an article, that read. Who is this mysterious CEO A. A Tucker? What does he look like?"

The article went on to say that the mysterious CEO, appoints a figurehead to take the heat while he goes undercover, to scope out the company he wants to take down or land he wants to buy for profit. The article gave a sample of his handwriting.

Sylvia took a sip, of her tea, studying the flamboyant signature, and muttered, "I've seen that hen scratching before." She took out the note Harry found on Sid, then, tried to match it with one of the ranch hands. She then, shouted, "Bingo! Now I know, who you are." She picked up Flash and said, "You be my guard Flash while I take a shower." and placed the cat on the bed.

In the shower, Sylvia heard the cat growling, turned off the water and heard footsteps. Sylvia stepped out of the shower, crept across the bedroom to see who it was, then tripped and fell on the floor just as the room was peppered with bullets. Sylvia lay motionless, face down as she heard someone enter the bedroom, kick her in the side, and left.

Moments later, Bruce rushed in, as Stubs, Herb, and Harry, stood by the door. Bruce quickly covered his wife then checked, to see if she was alive. Sylvia lay still as she whispered, "Close the door." She then told him who Tucker was and stated, "Remember, I'm dead."

Bruce pulled the blanket over his wife's head, opened the door and said, "It's time I took down that Slimeball Tucker. Stubs, you stay here with the lumbermen Herb, Harry you two come with me."

Forty-five minutes later, Bruce approached Tucker's secretary's desk and said, "I'm here for Tucker."

The secretary pointed to the door, but, never announced him. Bruce barged in the office, and roared, "A. A. Tucker, you are under arrest, for the murder of the building inspector, and Sid."

"You can't pin that rap on me. I was out of town during both murders and I can prove it."

Bruce stared at Herb, and said, "But, you weren't, Mr. Tucker."

In mock innocence, Herb quickly replied, "The strain has finally gotten to you, Bruce. I'm your hired ranch hand, not some CEO of this corporation."

"You are my hired hand alright, disguised as Tucker so you can perform your famous squeeze play on me to force me off my land."

The fake Tucker behind the desk, slowly opened the top desk drawer, slid his hand in, took hold of a gun, but, before, he could fire, a bullet from Harry's gun struck him in the chest.

"But I am not, A. A. Tucker," affirmed Herb.

Duncan walked in, with two of his men dressed in dark gray suits, and stated, "Thanks Marshall Bruce, you've done a great job." he turned to Herb, and said, "You are definitely, A. A. Tucker, alias the Chameleon. Now, you will be known by a number." Duncan glanced at Bruce, and said, "We'll clean up here."

The secretary poked her head in the office, and asked, "Is that a wrap, Duncan?"

"Not quite Kitty, we still have to catch one who was pulling Tuckers' strings and thanks to you. Oh, don't forget to tell Connie and Mosey that I need them here."

On a Saturday morning weeks later, Sylvia woke, walked around, with just a thin bathrobe on, made herself a cup of tea for herself, coffee for her husband, and questioned, "Are you, going to tell me what you are doing behind that stockade fence out back?"

Dressed, Bruce took his coffee from his wife, led her outback, unlocked the gate, and showed her the gazebo she wanted to build and said, "We'll finish the flagstone walkway Monday. What do you think?"

Sylvia entered the edifice, and said, "I love the white scrollwork, the padded benches, and the plush rug on the floor."

Bruce stood by a small panel and explained, "I also installed speakers, for soft music, lights for the night, and shades for privacy. What do you think?"

Sylvia examined the panel and asked, "Can you play some nature sounds like the surf crashing on the shore?"

Sylvia turned on the sounds of pounding surf, lowered the blinds, stepped out of her robe, saying, "Now, we have the time and the place. Come here."

CHAPTER 13 TUMULT

A week later, Bruce walked in the bedroom of an ultra-modern home In Wickenburg with Detective Ken. A pudgy man in his fifties, with short light Brown hair, dressed in a white shirt and tan pants. Stared down, at a voluptuous young woman lying on the floor, with long, light brown wavy hair, in her mid-twenties, clad in a white negligee, with a long thin knife in her chest.

Ken stated, "I don't know why the captain wants you here. It's a simple open and shut case. The woman killed herself because her boyfriend left her."

Bruce examined the woman and questioned, "What about these contusions on her hips and stomach? I think someone forced himself on her then killed her."

Ken picked up the suicide note, written in the woman's own handwriting, that read, "Now that Tom doesn't want any part of me, there is no use in living any longer."

Bruce studied the note, picked up the King James Bible, on her nightstand, and opened to the first page, and read, I gave my life to Christ, on January 14, 1990. An application to attend B.T. Bible School fell out of the Bible and landed at the Detective Ken's feet. He picked it up, read, it and said, "Just because she planned to attend a Bible School doesn't mean anything."

Bruce sighed, then, stated, "The woman was a born-again Christian, she could not have killed herself, she was murdered."

Detective Ken threw his hands up in the air, and grumbled, "Alright! The case is yours! I am out of here."

Bruce took out his cell phone, called, and asked, "I need your help, in solving a murder. I'm at 225 North Jack Burden Road. How soon can you get here?"

Patrick and Alexis walked in the bedroom, and asked, "Is this fast enough?"

"How'd you do that?"

Patrick stared at the woman, and hollered, "Whoa! This does not look good! Alexis, check out the e-mails on her computer while I examine the body."

Patrick placed his green bag next to the woman's side, took out a metal plate, placed each of her hand, on it, then, uploaded the woman's fingerprints into his laptop. Examined the bruises on her body. He slowly scanned the room, then at the knife sticking out of the woman's chest. Took hold of the knife to remove it, and muttered, "The knife in this poor woman's chest is past the hilt. No one stabbed her she walked into the killer's trap. Here, I'll show you." Patrick pulled the knife out, and explained, "Notice, that the knife resembles a dart more than a knife." Patrick walked across the room to a bookshelf, lifted up a section of mock books to reveal a small cannon. Then, stated, "My guess is after her shower, she came into her bedroom, stepped on the microswitch hidden under the rug, firing the knife out of the cannon, killing her."

"Microswitch?" questioned Bruce.

"I haven't found it yet but I am sure I will."

"What are those contusions on her body?"

Patrick picked up a piece of plastic, and said, "This was used as wadding in the cannon. When the cannon fired, the plastic wadding struck her."

Bruce covered the woman with a bedsheet, sat on the bed and said, "I am way in over my head on this one."

Alexis walked into the room and stated, "Nothing unusual about her computer. She was working on a novel, had plenty of friends. Tom did leave her, but, it was an understanding between them, that things were not working out. Oh, her name was Sasha C. Dixon, age 24, she taught Sunday School, and she was in the church choir."

Bruce examined the small cannon, and inquired, "Just an 'off the wall' question; "Could Sasha have rigged the cannon herself, to make it look like somebody murdered her?"

"I doubt it. That cannon was homemade, and Sasha's hands are soft. If she was used to using a welding torch, her hands would show it. Besides, there isn't a tig welder on the premises."

"I might as well call the morgue," stated Bruce.

"Don't bother, Alexis and I will tidy up."

"Oh. One more thing," stated Bruce, "What about the suicide note? Did the killer return to the scene of the crime and leave the note?"

"I'll meet you at your place this evening and fill you in on my findings."

As Bruce was leaving, he met a tall thin man in his twenties walking up to the house, and asked, "Is Sasha in trouble?"

"And you, are?"

"I'm Tom. I dropped by to give her some CD's that she left at my place."

A feeling of hopelessness gripped Bruce, as he searched for the words to tell Tom, about Miss Dixon's fate. Then asked, "Would you like something cold to drink?"

"Sure would, Sasha always keeps a good supply of coke in the fridge."

Sitting in the living room, Bruce took a swallow of his drink, and said, "Tom, I am sorry to tell you, Miss Sasha C. Dixon has been murdered."

Stunned by the news, Tom dropped his coke, and cried, "No! That can't be true! I just spoke to her a few hours ago!"

"A neighbor found her body and called the police. Do you mind if I ask you a few questions?"

"No. Go ahead."

"Was Miss Dixon ever depressed, to the point that she would take her own life?"

"No. Sasha was an energetic Christian, in love with the Lord. Why do you ask?"

"There was a note found, on the nightstand, that said, she could not live without you."

"Can I see her?"

"Sure. Follow me."

Tom fell to his knees, with tears streaming down his face, as Bruce lifted up the bedsheet.

Tom sat on the bed, and asked, "Do you know who did it?"

"No. How close were you to Miss Dixon?"

"We dated for six months then, we decided to split up but, we never got into sex. But Sasha never warns anything that was revealing, let alone thin nightclothes."

"How do you know what Sasha wore to bed if you didn't sleep with her?"

"I have visited Sasha in the mornings when she had on her long cotton nightgown and bathrobe."

Patrick interrupted, "Not to change the subject, but, would you happen to know of someone who does tig welding? my camper needs some work."

Bruce shook his head, and stared at Tom, he quickly replied, "Don't look at me. The fumes from that thing make me gag."

Bruce stated, "Tom, don't say anything to anyone about, Miss Dixon's murder.

"Oh ah, Sasha had no family, that I know of." Bruce escorted Tom to his car then he left for home heavyhearted.

Home, Bruce parked his burgundy, SUV on the left side of the house, and sat in one of the cedar Adirondack chairs on the porch. Sylvia poked her head out of the door and asked, "Why didn't you come inside? I have a surprise for you."

"Not now, Sweet."

"Who rained on your parade today?"

"I don't want to talk about it."

Sylvia glanced around, snuck outside, clad in a thin nighty that went down to her hips, sat on her husband's lap and said, "I missed you today."

"I am in no mood this evening; all I want to do is sit here and be quiet."

Sylvia reached under Bruce's arms to tickle him. He pushed her away, sending Sylvia down on her butt. She sprang to her feet, stuck her finger in his face, stating forcefully, "I am not going to stop bugging you until you tell me what is bothering you."

Bruce rubbed his wife's side, saying, "I am sorry if I hurt you. I am having a hard time believing what happened today. Hey, you'd better put something on. Patrick and Alexis will be here any minute."

"I didn't tell you to stop rubbing my side. You are going to take a shower, then, I am going to give you a back rub to loosen you up. Then you are going to tell me, what has you down in the dumps."

In the shower, as Sylvia washed Bruce's back, he stated, "Do you remember a Miss Sasha C. Dixon, who goes to our church?"

"Sure do. She is the little ball of fire who goes around helping everyone. Why?"

"Somebody murdered her today then tried to make it look like a suicide."

"You're kidding. Tell me, you are kidding me, Bruce."

"I wish I was. A neighbor found her on the bedroom floor with a knife in her chest."

"Was it a forced entry?"

"No. Someone set up a small cannon triggered by a microswitch when she stepped on it, the cannon shot the knife into her chest, killing her."

"No wonder you're down. That news took the gimp right out of me too. Have you told Pastor Giles yet?"

"No. he and his wife are away until tomorrow evening."

"Has Connie, Mosey and Kitty got here yet?"

"Not yet but they should soon."

As Sylvia and Bruce were getting out of the shower, a knock came to the front door. Sylvia shouted, "Just a minute!" threw on a pink sundress, and answered the door, and asked, "Can I help you, Detective Ken?"

"Is your husband here?"

"He'll be out in just a minute. Would you like a cup of coffee while you are waiting? It's French Vanilla cream."

"Sounds great."

Bruce helped himself to a mug of coffee, and asked, "Ken. What brings you, out here to my ranch?"

"The captain is ticked off at you. What did you do? The house where the body was, is immaculate, and the body is missing. It's not in the house it's not in the morgue. Where is It?"

"Sergeant Ben is not my boss; therefore, I do not have to answer to him. Everything is, as it should be."

"Try telling that to the Sergeant, who is about to put your head, on the chopping block."

"Sergeant Ben is an associate, no more, no less. If he wants any information about this case, he is going to have to call Duncan."

"Who is this Duncan guy? If you are talking to someone about this case outside this jurisdiction you are in so much hot water."

Bruce asked Ken to follow him to the barn, there, he picked up a pressure treated two by twelve, stood it against the fence outside, picked up a rock, walked back ten steps, turned, and threw the rock at the plank, putting a hole in it. Then, he stated, "I do not work for Sergeant Ben, I work for Duncan. If Ben wants to put my head on the proverbial chopping block, because I don't dance to his beat, he is welcome to try, but, he's the one who will wind up in trouble, not me."

Detective Ken stared at Bruce, then at the hole, with his mouth open in shock and asked, "Who are you?"

"Just, someone on the side of law and justice that's all you need to know. Oh ah, one more thing, Ken. Don't go spreading around, about my abilities. Okay?"

Patrick drove up in his jeep, with Alexis, and watched Ken speed off, wondering what was chasing him. Patrick hollered, "I have the forensic report already?"

In the house, Patrick gave Bruce the report saying, "Miss Sasha C. Dixon was 24 years old, five feet nine inches tall with no viable scars anywhere on her body. She was not molested before she was killed, and the bruise was from the plastic wadding in the cannon. Outside of that, Miss Dixon lived an active life in the church, with plenty of friends.

The cannon was made from two-inch aluminum tubing, that used smokeless black powder, with a wireless triggering device."

"Did the lab find any clues, that might tell us, who the killer might be?"

"They came up with nothing."

"Do you think this may be the start of a serial killer?"

"That is a possibility, oh and here is a list of her friends that you want to question."

Sylvia gave Bruce the phone whispering, "It's Sergeant Ben."

"I didn't hear the phone ring."

"I had it on low so it wouldn't disturb you and Patrick, but, Ben demanded to speak to you."

Bruce turned on the speaker then, answered, "What can I do for you, Sarge?"

"I will not have any mavericks running around my district is that clear? If, you value your job be in my office within the hour! Is that clear?"

"But, Sir, do you know what time it is?"

"I don't care if it is midnight! Be here!"

Bruce hung up the phone, and stated, "I don't believe this guy. Where does he get off telling me what to do?"

Patrick stated, "The first thing tomorrow morning, you are going to see, what Sergeant Ben wants. But, Duncan will be there to meet you. Now, how about a mug of coffee, and a mess of Sweet Rolls?"

"I'll get the coffee and goodies," stated Sylvia, "And meet you two in the gazebo."

Alexis asked, "Sylvia. Do you mind if I pet the horses?"

"Help yourself."

Twenty-two minutes later, Harry approached the gazebo, carrying Alexis, with an arrow in her shoulder.

Patrick quickly questioned, "What happened?"

"One minute, she was petting Sylvia's horse, then she was on the hay screaming with an arrow stuck in her with this note attached to it."

Bruce opened the note, and read, "This is just a warning. The one Tucker was working for still wants your ranch and will have it sooner or later, so don't get involved with this case."

"You didn't see anyone?" inquired Bruce.

"Nope."

Harry placed Alexis face down on the gazebo deck, as Patrick asked, "Sylvia, get me brown medical bag from the back of me jeep." He turned to Alexis, and said, "Hang in there."

Two minutes later, Patrick took his bag from Sylvia, opened it, took out a laser scalpel, and cut open Alexis's blouse, and studied the arrow wound. Sighed and stated, "There is no way I can remove that arrow with what I have." Patrick gazed at Alexis, and said, "Love, I'm afraid I am gonna have to push the arrow through. Okay? I'll give you something for you to bite down on."

Patrick asked Bruce, "Hold her by her shoulders, Sylvia hold her legs down, so, she doesn't kick," Patrick took a firm grip, on the arrow and shoved. Alexis shrieked in agony as Patrick tried to comfort his love saying, "Just a little bit more, you are doing good Alexis. That's it, we are done."

Harry knelt down, and said, "You are one brave lady. I know many a grown man that would have passed out."

"Really," replied Alexis, in a soft voice.

As Patrick was bandaging Alexis, Mosey, a 5 ft 5 inch tall oriental woman in her early twenties with a black belt in karate. Connie, a five foot five, 25 year-old woman, with short brown hair with an attractive perky figure, and Kitty, a 35 year old woman, 5 feet 9 inches tall with short curly dark brown hair, approached the gazebo. Bruce stated, "The men's bunkhouse is empty, so you ladies can sleep there. Don't worry each bed has its own room with a dresser and a nightstand. Dinner is at five o'clock."

Connie inquired, "Is there anything we can do to help?"

"Thank you for asking but we'll be fine."

CHAPTER

14 A CHALLENGE

The next morning, Bruce entered Sergeant Ben's office and asked, "You wanted to see me, Sergeant Ben?"

"Shut the door behind you and sit-down," growled Ben.

With the door closed, Bruce sat in the Sergeant chair, folded his arms across his chest, and stated, "Sergeant Ben everything concerning this case, is no longer in your hands. So, get off my back before I am forced into doing something you will regret."

"I told you to be in my office last night, get out of my chair, and who are you to order me around? I want to know what happened to that woman›s body, and the evidence you found at the crime scene!"

"That›s on a need to know basis and you don›t need to know."

"You insubordinate piece of garbage! If you don›t tell me what you did, with that body right now I›ll have you thrown in prison for interfering in a police investigation, withholding evidence, and accessory to murder!"

"I don›t think so, Sergeant." stated Bruce, stood on his feet, slammed his fist on the mahogany desk, split it in half, picked up Ben and stated through clenched teeth, "You are beginning to get under my skin."

Duncan entered the office, with two well-dressed men in gray suits, and stated calmly, "Bruce, put Sergeant Ben down."

Duncan walked up to Ben, fixed his collar saying, "Bruce works for me, not you. All the information you have in this silent killer case is to be given to my man Bruce."

"But, Sir. This is my district; Bruce is just a Marshall."

"Just, a Marshall?" questioned Duncan, "Check, again. Bruce›s jurisdiction is wherever I send him. Give Bruce any more trouble, and I›ll come down on you, like a Mac truck."

Back at the ranch, Sylvia introduced the new cleaning lady. Barbara a thirty-five-year-old woman, with a perky figure, dark brown curly hair, clad in hot pants, a white, low cut top, and. She smiled, at Bruce, gave him a boob crushing hug, saying, "Glad to meet you. If there is anything, you need, just let me know." then for the next forty minutes Barbara monopolized Bruce›s attention until Sylvia interrupted, "Ah, Barbara, can you start by cleaning the kitchen?"

"Sure, oh, do you have a cleaning cloth?"

Barbara went into the kitchen, and cleaned, while Bruce scooped out the ashes in the fireplace while drinking his coffee. Ten minutes later, Barbara walked in the living-room, faced Bruce, and said, "I have this nice bathing suit, that I bought yesterday," and promptly bent over. He took a swallow of his coffee, knelt to finish his job, ignoring Barbara's advances. Sylvia stared at her husband's uncomfortable situation, and asked, "Barbara could you help me fold some clothes in the laundry room?"

As Barbara was cleaning the bathroom down the hallway, Bruce asked, "Sylvia. Where in the world did you find that flirt?"

"Pastor Giles highly recommended her. He said that she is a good worker, modest, and someone I can trust. What happened this morning, with Captain Ben?"

"Duncan read him the Riot Act. Then, told him that he is to report to me."

"I bet that went over like a lead balloon."

Harry walked in the front door as Barbara entered the living-room from the hall, glanced at her skimpy attire, shook his head in disgust, went into the kitchen for a cold glass of water, bumped into Barbara, and dumped his cold water down the front of her blouse. She squealed, "Oh, that is cold!" Turned to Sylvia, and asked, "Do you mind if I leave early so I can change my top?"

"Go, ahead. I›ll see you tomorrow around the same time and wear something modest."

Sylvia watched Barbara leave, looked at Harry, and said, "You did that on purpose didn›t you?"

"The little filly needed to cool down if you know what I mean."

"What›s up, Harry?"

"I just herd over my scanner that there has been another murder at, 141 East Genung Avenue, in Wickenburg."

Bruce kissed his wife goodbye, and said, "Let›s go, Harry. Hopefully, we can get there before they do."

At a ranch house, where the murder took place, Bruce and Harry, ducked under the yellow police line tape, an officer questioned, "Where do you think you two are going?"

Bruce showed the officer his ID and said, "He›s with me." and entered the house. Bruce approached Detective Ken, and inquired, "What do we have?"

"Miss Lillie Foster, white female, mid-twenties, about one hundred and thirty pounds, blond hair, with a knife, stuck in her back."

Bruce entered a large powder blue-tiled bathroom with a matching sink, tub, and toilet. Pulled back the shower curtain, and studied the body of the dead woman, lying face down in the bathtub full of water. He emptied the water from the tub, checked the dead woman›s body for contusions, lifted her right shoulder, and found a red, smartphone, handed it to Harry to catalog. He tapped the knife sticking out of her back, with his finger, before pulling it out. Bruce stood up, took a bath towel, off the toilet, covered the woman, and asked, "Was there a suicide note with this one too?"

Detective Ken handed Bruce a note that read, my life isn›t worth living So, I have set up a trap so I can kill myself." Bruce shook his head muttering, "This does not make sense. Knelt by the tub, lifted the bathmat and found a micro switch. Glanced across the bathroom to the towels stacked on a shelf. Hidden among the towels was a small, homemade cannon, that used smokeless black powder. Bruce ordered, "Harry, check to see if there are any voice mails."

Patrick entered the bathroom, lifted the towel, and muttered, "Not another young lassie. You, Ken, help Bruce bring her into the bedroom and put her on the bed so I can examine her."

"You›re going to do an autopsy here?" questioned the Detective.

"Duh! I›m going to do a preliminary exam. Now, if you would be so kind, as to make yourself useful and get us all coffee. This is going to be a long one."

Harry entered the bedroom with a digital recorder, and said, "You have got to hear this, Boss, it was left in the voice mail."

"Let›s hear it."

A woman›s voice was heard sobbing, "To anyone hearing this. I am scared. There is a strange man going around, checking certain people to see if they want to be in the movies. He drives a white van, with black smudges on the right side." the phone suddenly went dead.

Patrick inquired, "Did you find anything else, Harry?"

"Nope, the house is clean. No prints, shoe marks nothing."

"I›m having second thoughts about those black and blue marks, on the woman›s body."

"Oh, Why?"

There were some marks on her back, and rump, but, there are a few on her chest, shoulders, and hip as well. To me, it appears that she was beaten before she was murdered."

A woman in her fifties walked in the bedroom, and demanded, "What are you people doing in my daughter›s bedroom, and where is Lillie?"

Bruce sighed, and said, "I am sorry ma›am, your daughter was murdered."

"That can›t be true!" screamed the mother.

Patrick lifted the bed sheet, and asked, "Is this your daughter?"

The mother went into hysterics, over the death of her daughter. Patrick ordered, "Hold her down so I can give her a shot!"

After the shot, Bruce placed the mother on the sofa and left.

Ken returned with the coffee, Harry got in Ken›s face, and inquired, "What evidence did you remove from the scene before we arrived?"

"Get out of my face!" shouted Ken.

"I know you›re withholding evidence because no crime scene can be this clean."

Bruce walked up to the mother and asked, "Mrs. Bower, do you know if your daughter had enemies?"

"She was a quiet girl and I can›t think of anyone who wanted to kill her."

"Do you know anything about a white van?"

"My daughter sounded a bit nervous the past few days, but, she wouldn't tell me what was wrong."

"Warn everyone you know that if they see a white van with black smudges on the side, call the police right away."

Two men wearing white smocks entered the bedroom and ordered, "Okay, everyone out."

Bruce stated, "I›ll see you later. Oh, Alexis is doing better."

Back at the ranch, Bruce asked, "Stubs, how's the wind generators doing?"

"All of them are working perfectly, Sir. Do you mind, if I take off early? Because I want to soak my back. It›s been bothering me, lately."

"Sure, go ahead. I›ll see you tomorrow morning."

Bruce gave his wife a kiss and said, "I›ll be in the barn." He set up the cannon from the first murder, loaded it, and fired the knife at the barn wall, with little effect.

Patrick, came by later, saw Bruce fooling around with the cannon and asked, "What'cha doing?"

"I don›t think those girls were killed with this cannon. Watch." Bruce loaded the cannon inserted the knife, and fired, the knife flew through the air, and stuck about an inch in the barn wall."

"I see what you mean."

Harry poked his head in the barn door, and said, "I›m gonna stay in the bunkhouse until these murders are solved."

Bruce showed Harry what the cannon can do, and questioned, "How do you think, the women were murdered?"

"Well Sir, Miss Phillip›s hair was done up, like she was going to a ball; what if some sicko is going around promising young women, fame, and fortune, set the cannon up as a prop. Then the murderer tells the woman that he is going to play the killer. The woman has stars in her eyes as she steps in front of the camera only to be stabbed to death. Then the killer sets up the cannon and leaves some whacked out suicide note, to throw us off the track."

"Sounds possible," remarked Patrick.

Bruce walked in the house wanting to collapse, when Sylvia exited the bedroom wearing a thin red negligee, placed her arms on his shoulders and said, "I know just what you need."

"Ah, Hon, I am not up for fooling around. It has been one long day."

"I know. Trust me, on this. Now, go into the bedroom and get ready for a back rub you will never forget."

Sylvia entered the bedroom, sat on the bed, and poured lotion on her husband's back and began to rub. Bruce questioned, "Where did you get that stuff from? I like the smell."

"Patrick gave it to me. He said that it is an old family recipe. When I finish your back, I›ll do the rest of you as well. Hello, Bruce. Husband of mine. Are you with me?"

All Sylvia heard was her husband snoring. She stared at him and muttered, "I am not going to wake him. He›ll have to sleep that way." Sylvia locked the front door, hung her negligee on the bedroom door, crawled in bed with her husband and was fast asleep in no time. The next morning, they were wakening by a constant knocking on the door. Sylvia grumbled, "Oh, Crap. That's Barbara."

Bruce stated, "You get dressed, while I answer the front door and tell her that we will be up in a few minutes."

"Put some clothes on!" whispered Sylvia loudly.

"I›m not going to let her in dressed like this. Give me some credit will you please."

Bruce opened the front door a crack, smiled sheepishly and said, "Barbara it›s so nice to see you. Can you give us a few minutes."

Barbara pushed the door open, and marched in clad in her usual skimpy attire, stared at Bruce, and said, with a sparkle in her eyes, "My, you›re looking good today Bruce. Don›t worry we›re friends so it is alright if I see you that way."

Bruce picked up the throw on the couch, wrapped it around himself, and stated, "Why don›t you wait outside?"

"If you don›t mind I›ll start cleaning the living room."

"I mind you drooling all over my husband." bellowed Sylvia from the bedroom doorway dressed in her bathrobe. There are several loads of dirty clothes that need to be washed."

"I thought I would start cleaning the living-room first if it›s alright with you."

Sylvia held her temper, walked up to Barbara, took hold of her arm, and forcefully turned her around. Then, marched her out into the laundry room.

Dressed, Bruce entered the kitchen, took out some eggs, sausage, English muffins, and potatoes, for home-fries to cook breakfast.

Barbra walked into the kitchen a few minutes later, and stated, "Oh, I love sausage and eggs."

"You think I›m cooking up hen eggs and pig sausage? My wife and I are having ground snake meet and lizard eggs. You want some?"

Barbara quickly put her hand to her mouth, and rushed to the bathroom, with Bruce chuckling to himself.

Sylvia tapped her husband›s side saying, "Why did you tell her that?"

"It›s payback for barging in when I wasn't dressed." He glanced down at his wife and asked, "Are you gonna go commando today?"

"You›re not going to let me live that down are you."

"Nope. Come here wife of mind and kiss me."

"I need to get dressed," Bruce patted his wife›s back saying, "You and me later."

"You wish."

Bruce wrapped his arms around Sylvia, kissed her and said, "I need to give you a back rub tonight."

"Can we discuss this when Big Ears Barbara isn›t around," whispered Sylvia.

Alexis wandered into the kitchen in a short, yellow-flowered nightgown, and asked, "Can›t a body get any sleep around here?"

"How›s your shoulder?" inquired Bruce.

"It›s feeling better, but I still have a bit of stiffness in my arm, smiled devilishly and said, "Be right back and returned wearing a pair of pixie wings. Barbara returned, saw Alexis standing in the middle of the kitchen with her wings slowly flapping and exclaimed, "Omygosh! Sylvia, you have a huge pixie standing in your kitchen!"

"Pixie?" questioned Sylvia, "Where?"

"That woman standing right in front of you!"

"You mean Alexis? She is short, but she does not have wings."

"Are you two blind, or something? Her wings are coming right out of her back!"

Sylvia suggested, "Barbra. Why don›t you go into the bathroom and splash some cold water on your face, then I›ll fix you some breakfast."

As soon as Barbara left the room, Sylvia instructed, "Alexis, get rid of your wings."

"What, not in front of your husband."

"This is no time for modesty. The last thing you need is to be plastered all over tomorrow's newspaper."

Alexis took off her nighty hung it on the back of the chair, trying to cover herself, as Sylvia assisted in removing the fake wings," When Barbara returned, she saw Alexis sitting at the table, eating her eggs sausages and potatoes, walked in back of her and inquired, "Where are your wings?"

Alexis gazed at Barbara and asked, "What are you talking about lady?"

"Before I went into the bathroom, you had wings sticking out of your back."

"Ma›am, have you been smoking locoweed? If I had wings, I would not be hanging around this dry barren state, that›s for sure."

Barbara sat at the table and said, "I need a good strong cup of coffee right now. I could have sworn you had wings."

Sylvia asked, "Barbara, why don›t you take the rest of the day off."

Mosey, Kitty, and Connie entered the kitchen, sat at the table and had their breakfast. Bruce gave them a list of names and said, "Two women were murdered, here are their named and who they knew. I want you guys to talk to them and see what you can come up with. Oh, and here are the folders of the victims. You will be paid, twenty dollars an hour for your time."

CHAPTER 15 TOO CLOSE FOR COMFORT

Bruce kissed his wife saying, "I'm going with Harry, and Stubs to check the wind generators. I'll see you at suppertime."

Sylvia asked Alexis. "Do you want me to help you to get dressed? Or do you want to hang around in your nightshirt?"

"The statusquo is fine, if you don't mind."

"You want to join me in the gazebo?" questioned Sylvia.

"Sure. How about a cup of hot Chamomile tea, and pastry?"

In the gazebo out back, Alexis took a sip of her tea and asked, "Sylvia. Tell me how you met Bruce?"

Sylvia smiled and said, "Bruce was picking up people from the local long-term hospital where I was. I rolled up to him in my wheelchair in my cotton blue dress with red flowers and asked him if he could take me to church. He wheeled me out to my car and took me to the first service that starts at 7th AM. After church, he stopped off at DD's where we had lunch and he brought me back to the hospital. The rest is history."

"Did you two ever mix it up before you were married?" questioned a curious Alexis.

"We cuddled on the bed once or twice but nothing big.

Alexis eyes sparkled as she stated, "Before I met Patrick, I loved to walk around in my hot pants and halter top just having a ball. One morning I climbed a tree and wound up in a mess. I hollered for an hour trying to free myself, and the only thing I managed to do was tire myself out. Patrick came by, looked up and asked, "You need a hand getting free?"

Of course, smart mouth me, answered, "No, I like hanging around trees tangled up in vines." Patrick watched me struggle for a few more minutes than asked, "Are you sure you don't need any help?"

I snapped back, "Do, I look like I need your assistance? he cut me out of the vines anyways."

"You're knight in shining armor came to rescue you. How romantic." stated Sylvia Alexis hung her head and said, "I know I should have said no, when Patrick, stepped in the shower with me. But I ran out of the shower convicted over what I was going to get into with him. Patrick then walked out of my life until we met Him and Jade in your cave."

Sylvia placed a reassuring hand on Alexis shoulder and said, "You have got to stop condemning yourself for what you did back then and go on. It is in the past, ask His forgiveness and move on in Christ. I've done plenty of things that I am not proud of but, repent before Christ and vow not to do it again."

Just as Alexis bent over for a doughnut, an arrow embedded itself in the post behind her. She dove for the floor, and Sylvia hit the switch lowering the heavy shades. Then peeked out of the blind, and said, "Whoever it was must be in the house.

Just then the gazebo blinds began to raise, Sylvia muttered, "He found the switch, duck." Another arrow caught the side of Alexis's nightshirt, as she dove for the floor. And asked, "Did you see who it was?"

"No, all I saw was a black shadow."

Just then they heard Flash howl as it attacked someone. Moments later, A trail of dust followed a car, as it raced out the road.

Sylvia and Alexis rushed through the house and fastened their eyes on the speeding vehicle trying to figure out who it was. When they heard footsteps behind them coming their way. Alexis whispered, "If we both jump him, I think we can overpower him."

"On the count of three."

Standing directly behind the women, Patrick asked suddenly, "What's up?"

Sylvia let out a scream and jumped, as terrified Alexis squealed, "Patrick! You scared me within an inch of my life. Don't do that ever again! Now, I have to change my undies, Thanks a lot!"

"What did I do?" questioned Patrick.

Sylvia explained, "Someone took another shot at Your wife. Thanks to Flash he chased him off. What have you found out about the two murderers so far?"

"There is never a sign of a struggle, no forced entry, and there was not enough power in the cannons to killed those two women. I think some sicko is posing as a movie director, promising these women fame, and fortune if they star in a murder scene, He tells the woman that he will play the part of the killer. This puts them off guard by setting up the cannon. During the filming he kills them."

"But, why" questioned Sylvia, "There has to be a connection somewhere. Jilted lover, revenge over some stupid incident, something."

Bruce returned, looked at Alexis then at his wife and inquired, "What happened?"

"Someone tried to kill Alexis."

Patrick asked, "Bruce. Do you mind if Alexis and I sleep in the bunk house until this is over?"

"Sure, go ahead." Bruce glanced at his wife and said, "How's barbecued ribs sound for dinner tonight?"

"As long as I don't have to cook them."

That evening, Harry approached Sylvia under the picnic shelter, kissed her and asked, "How are you this evening Mrs. B.?

"Good. But, tell me why you are wearing a six shooter?"

"You never can tell when that sicko will try again."

Part way through the supper, Harry, slowly slid his gun out of its holster, saying, "Don't move Boss. There is someone by the corner of the barn. Take my gun, act like that there is nothing wrong. Alexis, Stay out of sight." Harry, rose to his feet saying, "Well, I don't know about you folks, but I am going to call it a night." then left, and circled around coming up on the prowler from behind, grabbed and landed a blow to the person's jaw then brought the person back to the picnic shelter. Once in the light Harry exclaimed, "It's a woman!"

Bruce asked, "Sweet, check her for weapons."

The woman woke and hollered, "Where's my crossbow?"

Patrick got in the woman's face and demanded, "Why are you trying to kill me gal?"

"My name is Violet Patterson, and I'm a bounty hunter. I was told that your lady friend is wanted for murder, in Mississippi. I was also told that I would paid fifteen thousand dollars, for her death, and it didn't matter how I did it, long as she was dead."

"Do you have proof?" asked Bruce.

The woman pulled a piece of paper out of her pocket and handed it to Bruce. He looked at it and said, "Looks official, but Alexis is not wanted for murder in any state. Do you know the person that gave you this?"

"No, I received it in the mail, and when I went to call to verify the wanted information. The secretary told me that the information was correct. Oh, do you know of a Jade? There is a five thousand dollar reward for her."

"Someone is giving you false information." stated Harry, "Neither one of them are criminals."

"I don't care. I am taking her in, and that's final."

Alexis whispered to Patrick, "I think I need to show her who I really am."

"Okay, if you think it will work."

Alexis stated, "Miss Patterson. If you will give me a minute, I will show you that I am no murderer." Patrick escorted his wife into the barn and he came back alone. Violet asked, "Hey! What is this a double cross?"

Patrick pointed up and said, "No, Alexis is up there."

Violet gazed skyward at Alexis hovering just above her head, stated, "You're a pixie. But they're myth."

"Funny I don't feel like an urban myth." Alexis landed, walked up to the bounty hunter, and said, "Go ahead and touch my wings, you'll see that I am real."

Harry handed Viola some barbecued ribs and asked, "Are you familiar with the suicide murders that took place this past week?"

"Yes, Detective Ken was on the news, saying that the woman committed suicide."

Bruce showed Viola the knife and the cannon that was supposed to have killed the women and said, "This is the murder weapon. But, the cannon doesn't have the power to kill a mouse, let alone a full-grown woman."

"If I hear of anything I'll let you know. But, what about my reward money."

Then we kill her."

"Hey, wait a minute! I don't think I like where this conversation is going," protested Alexis."

Bruce explained, "We'll stage Alexis's death, Patrick, can you get me some blood?"

"I can do better than that. I have a trick arrow, that I can put inside Alexis's blouse, then pour the blood on her. Viola, you can take a picture. That should take care of any more bounty hunters."

"I'm good with that," stated Alexis, "Just make sure that it's not one of my favorite tops you pour blood on." Alexis went in the barn, took off her fake wings and posed for her death. After the bounty hunter had left with the photo, Bruce turned to Alexis and stated, "You'll have to stay on this ranch until this whole thing is solved."

"Deal!" hollered Alexis.

The next morning, at breakfast, Connie handed Bruce some notes saying, "The name of the first woman murdered was, Sasha C. Dixon; and she was 24 years old. Her parents, died when she was young. Her siblings are scattered around the US. Which is going to make it difficult to investigate her murder. Miss. Dixon had few friends but the people I spoke to could only say good about her."

"I'll start with pastor Giles," stated Bruce, "He should know something."

"I'm coming with you," stated Sylvia, "Patrick, can you and Alexis hang around the ranch house, and keep an eye on Betty until we get back?"

Later that morning, Bruce walked in the pastor's office with his wife and inquired, "Do you know anything about Miss. Dixon?"

"The only thing I know is, she was would be in the church parking lot before the service every Sunday morning and Wednesday night."

"Did she ever date someone by the name of Tom?"

"No. She kept to herself, a lot. My only question is, why would she kill herself when she had so much going for her?"

"She was murdered, but the killer made it look like she did herself in."

"The only person that I know anything about her would be her friend Abigail, but she is on vacation right now."

"Thanks pastor, my wife and I will see you in church on Sunday." On his way out of the church. Bruce saw a white van matching the description of the killers, pull in the driveway of a light blue ranch house three doors down. Bruce pulled his SUV to the side of the road, and overheard the man tell the young woman after she answered the door. "I'm the movie producer you talk to on the phone the other day. May I come in, so we can discuss your part in the upcoming murder mystery?"

Bruce rushed up to the man, and asked, "Are you a for real producer? Can I look over your manuscript?"

The man glared at Bruce and took off. The woman hollered, "You babbling idiot! You just blew my chance to be famous! Get out of here before I call the police!"

Bruce showed the tall, young voluptuous woman, with short black hair, his badge, and said, "I just might have saved your life."

"How do you figure that out."

"Can I come in, so we can talk?"

"Sure. I'm Paula. Would you like some coffee?"

"Yes, thank you."

Bruce sat in the leather armed chair in the living room, took a swallow of his coffee and said, "There is someone going around posing as a movie director, telling women that they are going to be in the movies but, wind up with a knife in them."

"He seemed like a nice man; you must have him mixed up with somebody else."

"No ma'am, I am not mistaken, he's the one. If he returns, call the police immediately."

"Didn't the news on the TV say that those two women committed suicide?"

"Yes, but the media is wrong."

"Thank you for the information, and I will be careful, But, I have to get my work done. Good Day sir."

CHAPTER 16 KITTENISH PAULA

Three days later, Sylvia walked out to the gazebo in the evening in her blue shorts and a halter top, gave her husband a glass of iced tea and said, "I received this notice in the mail."

Bruce opened the letter that read, "You are four months behind in your mortgage payments so the bank is foreclosing on your ranch. Bruce muttered, "How can the bank do that when I used the money I received from all those diamonds to paid for this land."

Sylvia asked, "Is someone still using the squeeze play to force you off your land? But that's not what's bothering you."

"Paula is what's bothering me. I know that a woman isn't going to take my advice. All she could think of was getting a part in the movies and has a flagrant disregard for her life."

"Let's pray that she sees the danger and runs in the opposite direction. Now, get your mind off the case and on to something more pleasant"

"Like you, perhaps?"

"That's a start. Let's pray."

After, Bruce took his wife in his arms to kiss her when Harry rushed up, and said, "Sorry to interrupt Sir, but, the pastor just called. He said that a white van has been parked in front of Paula's house for the past half hour."

Get Patrick, and let's go!"

"Hey, I'm coming with you!" shouted Sylvia.

Forty-five minutes later, Bruce brought his SUV to a screeching halt in the driveway of Paula's home and ordered, "Harry, you take them back, I'll take the front, Sylvia, cover my back, Patrick, stay put and pray I don't need your medical services."

With his gun drawn, Bruce opened the front door and hollered, "Paula? Are you alright?"

Harry entered the living room from the kitchen and reported, "Clear!"

Bruce ordered, "Harry, you check the bathroom, I'll check the bedroom, Sylvia, you take the basement, she has to be around here somewhere."

Bruce hollered from the bedroom, "Harry, Sylvia, come here!"

Harry charged in the room and asked, "What's up?"

"I found lots of blood on the floor by the bed, but no Paula."

Sylvia shouted from the basement, "No one down here!"

Sylvia walked up to her husband in the kitchen, pointed to a bloody doorknob to the garage, said, "She has to be out there."

That knob did not have blood on it when I came in the back door," stated Harry.

"Paula's probably scared out of her mind and thinks we're out to kill her. So, be careful. "As Bruce opened the door, Sylvia pointed to a pool of blood by the front car door. Sylvia stated, "Let me talk to her?" She knelt by the car, looked under and said, "Paula, it's alright to come out. We're here to help you."

Paula reached out a trembling hand from under the car, Sylvia pulled her out, saw Paula with blood all over her thin light blue negligee and hollered, "Harry get Patrick and call 911!"

Pastor Giles crept in the garage and asked, "Is there anything I can do to help?"

"Yes, talk to her and keep her calm, while I find something to stop the bleeding."

Patrick rushed in, knelt, cut the sleeve off her nightshirt and tended to the five-inch-long gash on her left arm, stating, "You're lucky to be alive. Why did you let that wacko in your house in the first place?"

"He sounded so convincing when he told me that I was going to play a murder victim in my bedroom. He set up the camera and told me to go into the bathroom, take everything off and put on the fancy nightie then walk to my bed. When I got to my bed to take off my nightie, I turned to ask him something. That's when I saw the knife in his hand. He grabbed me by the arm, spun me around. I knead him between his pockets, left my bathrobe in his hand, and tried to escape. That's when he sliced my arm. He caught me in the living room by the fireplace. I whacked him in the chest with the poker, and I think, I knocked the knife out of his hand." Paula paused for a moment then said, "I am not sure but, I think that guy is a woman in disguise or a wacko. Because when I hit him, I tore open his shirt, and he was wearing a bra."

Sylvia assisted Paula into the living room and asked, "Are you sure about that?"

"I should know what a bra looks like," stated Paula. "Would you like me to fix your people some coffee?"

"You don't have to bother."

"It's no trouble."

"Let me give you a hand," suggested Sylvia.

Just then the paramedics rushed in along with Detective Ken. Patrick walked up to them and said, "You guys are a day late, and a dollar short as usual. Doctor Patrick, at your service. The victim had a severe laceration on her left arm that I fixed. You are welcome to check her out. But you will see that she is fine."

"This is the fifth time that I've found you treating people at a crime scene," stated the paramedic, "If I catch you again you will be arrested." Then shoved Patrick out of the way. Harry blocked their path saying, "Gentleman. If you would have arrived when you're supposed to. Patrick here would not have to do your job. Now, turn yourselves around and go back out the door. Oh, and apologize to Patrick before you leave."

Detective Ken walked up to Paula, and asked, "Did you hire this man to kill you?"

"What are you babbling about? The guy tried to stab me!" screamed Paula.

"The past two murders the woman hired some wing nut to kill them. Ergo suicide."

"Look you halfwit Detective." grumbled Bruce, "Go play marbles on the free-way or something. There is a maniac out there killing women for pleasure. I don't need your half-baked ideas fowling things up."

"Look, any moron can see that those two were suicides. The note the cannon. It all ties in."

Bruce stated, "Those cannons didn't have the power to kill a rat let alone a human."

"Oh, Bruce, the captain told me to tell you that if you are caught removing any more evidence from the crime scene, he'll throw you in jail."

"Tell the captain to keep his mind on his job, and off my business."

Paula looked at Bruce, and asked, "Do you think it's safe for me to stay here alone?"

"No. Why don't you stay at my ranch. Oh, Detective Ken, if you need to ask Paula any more questions. Feel free to pay me a visit, and when you are finished snooping around, lock up for me will you."

"Let me pack a few things first," stated Paula.

Back at the ranch, Sylvia showed Paula the guest room, and where the bathroom was and said, "Barbara will be here tomorrow morning at ten o'clock to clean. You can give her a hand dusting the furniture."

The next morning, Sylvia quickly rose from her bed at seven sharp, dressed and made breakfast. Bruce moaned, "Why are you up and dressed so early? You usually walk around for an hour or so before getting dressed."

"With Paula around, I have to be proper. What do you want? Eggs, pancakes, cold cereal for breakfast?"

"How about you for breakfast? asked Bruce.

"Sorry, Love, I'm not on the menu. See you in a bit." Sylvia walked into the kitchen and found Paula sitting at the table, drinking a cup of coffee wearing nothing but a short yellow, nightshirt.

Sylvia gently inquired, "Paula. Don't you think that short, nightie is a little spicy for a family setting?

"I didn't think you would mind, it's what I always wear in the mornings around the house."

Sylvia heard her husband coming and nervously said, "Paula. Why don't you check out our gazebo? It is nice this time of the morning." she then sighed in relief as Paula made her way outside.

Bruce walked in the kitchen, and inquired, "You look a bit uptight. What's bugging you?"

"Paula, that's who."

Bruce glanced out the back window, and stated, "Ah, that woman is coming this way with a short nightie on. Never mind my breakfast, I'll grab a cup of coffee and check the north field today. See ya." Bruce kissed his wife and headed out the door in a flash.

Barbara walked in the front door clad in hot pants and a halter top, saw Paula entering the back door, the expression on Sylvia's face quickly stated, "Trust me, ma'am you do not want to walk around here like that. Not with all the men coming in and out of here all day long."

"I'll just stay out of the way. No big deal."

"Let me put it this way. You look like a high-priced call-girl," stated Barbra.

"What?" screamed Paula, "Are you looking for a fat lip?"

Barbara spotted a glass of ice water on the table and promptly dumped it down the front of Paula's nightie. She let out a shriek and grabbed a hand full of Barbara's hair, then brought her knee up, and connected with Barbra's chin, then rammed her fist into her stomach. Barbra grabbed Paula by the back of her nightie, and dragged her into the bathroom, threw her in the shower, and turned on the water, saying, "Cool your hormones woman, or I'll slap you silly."

"You'll do what?" screamed Paula?" and ripped Barbra's top.

Barbara got in Paula's face and stated strongly, "Mr. and Mrs. Birdson was kind enough to let you in their home, so have the decency to act right."

"Or what?" growled Paula.

"I'll kick your sorry butt all over this ranch."

Paula grabbed Barbara by her throat and the two wrestled on the shower floor kicking and punching each other. Bruce rushed in the shower with Sylvia to stop the two women and Bruce stated, "Settle down or I'll put the both of you over my knee and give you a good spanking."

"Promise," asked Paula smiling.

The next morning, Bruce was up, and dressed early, walked out into the kitchen, and found Paula leaning against the stove in her usual nightwear. Bruce calmly stated, "Get dressed, and come with me."

Paula threw on a thin lacy robe and asked, "Are you going to wash my back in the shower?"

"Just get dressed, pack your things and follow me." Bruce led Paula to the bunkhouse, opened the door to a long white corridor with dark wooden doors on both sides and stated firmly, "This is where you will be staying from now on. Pick a door that doesn't have a name on it, then print your name on the paper provided, and tack it to the door. The key to your door is on the dresser. Oh, that door at the end of the hall is the bathroom. Mealtimes are at nine, twelve, and five. After breakfast, my wife will give you a list of chores to do."

"You're putting me to work?"

"Yes, no one freeloads around here. And if I catch you walking around that Skippy attire you call clothing again. I'll have Detective Ken lock you up somewhere for protected custody, is that clear Miss Paula? One more thing, around here we attend church Sundays mornings and Wednesdays nights. You will be expected to go with us."

"But, I don't go to church."

"As long as you are staying here, you will attend church. If you start to make excuses you are out of here."

"If you throw me out the killer will find me?"

"Then do what you are told, and he won't."

"You can't tell me what to do."

"No, but, if you have listened to me in the first place you would not be in this predicament."

Paula loosened her bathrobe, so it hung open, and said, "I'm sorry Sir." hoping to get Bruce's attention.

Bruce tried to ignore Paula's figure as he stated, "Barbara will be out later, to show you what you are to do. Just think of work as a means to keep your mind off the killer."

Back in the kitchen, Bruce sat at the table eating his apple pancakes, Sylvia cooked, but, never said a word. Sylvia sat across from him, and asked, "You're bugged about something? Is it Paula again?"

"You guessed it? I told her that I would have her locked up for her protection if she kept up her lewdness. Then marched her out into the bunkhouse. I will not have her running around this house flashing her whatever!"

"Relax Sweet. I trust you. But not her. If you will excuse me. I'm going to have a little woman to woman talk with Paula."

Sylvia marched to the bunkhouse, and pounded on Paula's door and bellowed, "Paula, I want to have a talk with you! Now!"

Paula opened her door a crack and asked, "What do you want?"

"The house is off-limits to you from here on in!"

"Oh? I thought your husband was in charge."

"You are right about my husband!" shouted Sylvia, "So bat those fake eyelashes somewhere else!"

"Look! If Bruce says that I can go to the house, I will, and there is nothing you can do about it."

Two rooms down on the right, Patrick opened his door, and asked, "Ladies. Please keep it down to a dull rower."

"Sure Patrick," answered Sylvia, turned and landed a hard right cross to Paula's jaw sending her flying to the floor, out cold."

Patrick walked up and stared at Paula lying on the floor and said, "I'll get Alexis to tend to her. You lassie go back to the house."

"I'll stay with Paula until Alexis gets here."

Alexis poked her head out her room door and asked, "Did someone mention my name?"

"Yeah," answered Patrick, "Paula needs some medical attention and I think you should do it."

Alexis yawned, wandered in Paula's room, glanced down at her and exclaimed, "Whoa! I guess she does. She grabbed a sheet from off the bed and covered her. then demanded, "Patrick go back to our room. I'll take care of her."

"How about if I get breakfast ready for us, instead."

That evening around the supper table, Bruce glanced at Alexis and questioned, "Do you know where Paula is?"

"After I patched her up from Sylvia's handy work. I gave her a shot in her butt, which will keep her asleep for a long time. If Paula wakes, I'll give her another shot. Hey, it's better than having her walk around exposing herself,"

CHAPTER 17 WHEN PUSH COMES TO SHOVE

That evening, Sylvia stared at her husband and inquired, "You want to go for a walk?"

Bruce took Sylvia's hand, and the two of them strolled out the long dirt road to the highway. Bruce inquired, "Have you had any more flashbacks, or nightmares about Randy?"

"No. Thanks to the Lord. I followed what pastor Giles told me, and that is to receive my healing because Christ provided it for me through the finished work on the Cross, it is just that simple."

Bruce pondered his next question, and asked gingerly, "Did Randy ever go all the way with you?"

"He just saw me in my undies because something always interrupted him before he could do anything. Which I am very thankful for. If he had actually done it to me, it would have sent me over the edge emotionally. To put your mind at ease, Hon, I detested Randy. Of course, my subconscious kicked in and my fear of Randy came out in my sleep."

Sylvia put her arm around Bruce's waist, and stated, "Don't worry about Randy I probably infuriated him so much, that he didn't remember what I looked like. I've said this to you before, you are the only man for me and that's the way it is going to be. Hey, Randy is dead, and in the past, so forget it."

On their way back to the ranch, Sylvia paused, stared at a park bench under a well-constructed wooden lean-to in the middle of nowhere and inquired, "What pray tell is that doing there?"

"It's for us to sit, talk and watch the sunset. What do you think of it?"

"I'll tell you after I try it. Let's go."

Sylvia sat on the bench with her husband, stared at Bruce's face and inquired, "How are you doing with that 'Silent Killer' Murder case?"

"I've been too busy dealing with Paula's scantly attire, to think about anything else."

"In other words, your heart is not in it. If you want my advice, Paula's story doesn't add up. The killer figures out every angle before he entered the victim's house. Then he executes his plan with precision perfection and is careful not to leave any clues behind. Then, here comes Paula, who states that she outsmarted this clever killer, who left her house a mess. I don't think so. You found a home-made cannon, and a long, thin knife at both crime scenes that was cleaned immaculately. However, at Paula's place, there was no cannon, no thin knife, and the place was covered with blood, instead of being spotless. Not only that the two murder victims were Christians that attended Pastor Giles's church they were cheerleaders who were in competition and so was Paula. If you ask me, I think she is protecting someone."

"I think I'll have Patrick keep Paula sedated to keep her out of the way. I had Kitty investigate Miss Dixon and she was seeing Tom but broke it off because all he thought of was sports. Kitty talked to Tom and confirmed it. I want to check out Paula and her home for clues."

"I'll frisk Paula, thank you, then, I'm going with you to check out her home. You need someone who will keep you going forward."

"I like to work alone, thank you."

"You now have a partner, me. Like it or not."

"I don't think I like this setup."

"With my sharp analytical mind, and your brawn, we can crack this case."

"Who am I to argue? What do you think we should do next?" asked Sylvia.

"Like you said Hon, we need to check Paula's home for clues."

Sylvia cast a suspicious eye at her husband and inquired, "Were you attracted to Paula?"

"No comment. I'm just glad she is sedated and out of the way."

"Then what else is bothering you?"

"I am being pressured by someone who wants to force me off my ranch so that they can build a large shopping complex and I think Paula fits into that somewhere. Detective Ken is more of a problem every time he shows up at a crime scene. Then there is the Sargent who is trying to force me off the case."

Sylvia lay on the bench with her knees bent and her head in Bruce's lap, saying, "I am sorry that you are having so much trouble but, back to Paula, in other words, you were tempted."

"She was alluring yes, but not to the point that I forgot that I am a child of God and toss you aside for her."

"Hey, can you build a better three-sided shelter over this bench for shade? This way we can sit, watch the sunset."

"Consider it done. Hey, sit up, you have got to see this fantastic sunset."

Sylvia sat up, cuddled close to Bruce until the sun had slipped below the horizon.

Back at the ranch, Sylvia suggested, "Bruce, you want to take a look in Paula's room? Maybe we can find something that will tell us why she is running interference for the killer."

"Sound fine to me."

"I'll go in first to make sure Paula is decent." Sylvia peeked her head in Paula's room, and said, "She's good."

Bruce entered the small room, and suggested, "Sylvia, you check her dresser, I'll check the desk."

Ten minutes later, Sylvia reported, "Nothing here. How about you?"

"All I could find is her ID. Guess what? Her real name is Susan Paula Stevens. First thing tomorrow we go to her house and turn it upside down until we find some clues as to why she is running interference for the killer."

Late that evening, Detective Ken knocked on the ranch house door then boldly walked in, glared at Bruce, and stated, "I want to talk to you. Now!"

Bruce rose to his feet, and stated, "I didn't tell you to come into my house."

"I told you that I wanted to speak to you."

Bruce got in the Detective's face, and said, "Ken. I don't like your attitude; I don't like the way you push people around. In fact, I don't like anything about you, plus, you do not barge in my house shouting demands. Sylvia, open the door please."

Bruce picked up the Detective, and bodily threw him out the door, across the porch, and on the ground. The Detective stood up and stated, "You remember Sergeant Ben, don't you? He has ordered you off 'The Silent Killer case."

Harry walked up behind Ken, stuck his Winchester to his head, and warned, "Say one more word, and I'll splatter your brains. Now, get in your car and get." Harry fired a shot in the air and shouted, "Now!"

"You heard me. Stay away from the Silent Killer case!" warned Ken.

Harry opened Ken's car door and stuffed him in, as Bruce, stated, "You come around here again interfering with this investigation you will be thrown in jail, and Police Sergeant Ben will not be able to help you."

"You've been warned," grumbled Ken.

Bruce hauled the Detective half out the car window, and stated, "You interfere in my investigation one more time, and you will be in more trouble than you know. Now, get off my property."

Harry turned to Bruce, and queried, "Why is everybody protecting this killer?"

"I have no idea."

The next morning, Bruce was up early, hauled his wife out of bed and, said, "We have to get going. I'll get the others, while you whip up some food."

After breakfast, Bruce, ordered, "Stubs, look after the ranch, Alexis, make sure Paula is sedated. Patrick, do you have the search warrant for Paula's house?"

"Ready to go Boss."

A short time later, Bruce parked his SUV in the driveway of Paula's light blue ranch house. Sylvia announced as they stepped out of the vehicle, "I'll check the bedroom!"

Bruce suggested, "Good, each take a room, and look for anything that will tell us why Paula is running interference for the killer."

Three hours later, in Paula's living-room, Patrick held up a plastic baggy with a cigarette butt in it, and tubing that the cannons were made from, a drop of motor oil from the garage floor and a man's electric razor, and stated, "For someone who lives alone with a new car. I'd say she's had a male visitor quite often."

Sylvia stated, "Hon, I found this picture of a cheerleader squad on the fireplace mantel. Recognize anyone?"

"Yeah, the two women on the left were murdered."

"Take a closer look."

"Yeah, Paula isn't in the picture."

"I found a cheerleader outfit in her closet that matches the ones in the picture. I also checked Paula's checking account and last week she made quite a large deposit which means someone paid her to run interference."

"I want the names and addresses of all those cheerleaders."

Harry hollered, "We have company!"

Bruce stood up, and said, "Detective Ken, you are here for what reason?"

"You were warned to stay away from this case."

Bruce walked up to the Detective and said, "You're like fingernails on a blackboard." then laid him out on the living-room floor with a right cross to his jaw. Patrick glanced down at Ken, and stated, "I'll call Duncan, and have this piece of work taken care of. You guys can go."

Bruce's cell phone rang, he answered it saying, "What's up Duncan?"

"There has been another murder, on the North Jackson side of Wickenburg. I need you to get there ASAP."

"Will Do. Oh, can you send some of your boys to Paula's place to pick up Detective Ken for interfering in police business."

A short time later, Bruce stopped his SUV in front of a log cabin ranch style house, turned to his wife and said, "You stay here. Harry, you're with me."

"Oh no you don't, I am coming with you. Like it or not." stated Sylvia.

Bruce walked up to the house, met a woman in her mid-forties and said, "I'm Miss Martha, Smith and I live next door. Thank God you're here. Kim and I were to take a camping trip this weekend. I came over to see if she needed any help with packing, but she didn't answer when I knocked."

Bruce kicked the front door open and entered a rustic style living room with a black bearskin rug by the fireplace. There on the floor by the coffee table made from a cross-section of a tree was a young woman with long wavy light brown hair, clad in pink lingerie, with a knife in her chest. Bruce knelt next to the body, to checked to see if she was still alive. He opened her nightgown, and found the same contusions on the woman's body." Sylvia examined the bruises and said, "This woman was beaten before she was stabbed, who could have done such a horrible thing?"

Just then Kim's chest heaved up and down, Bruce tapped his smartphone saying, "Patrick, Get over here now! I have a white female, about five feet six, a hundred and thirty pounds with a knife in her chest!"

"Is she alive?"

"Just barely!"

"Be there in a minute."

Sylvia studied Kim's body and stated "The contusions are not from the fragment of a cannon blast. Have you found the cannon yet?"

"I think it's tucked between some books on the other side of the room, and from what I can see, the murderer did a clean sweep before he left."

Sylvia held up the photo of the cheerleaders pointed to the third from the left and said, "I think someone is killing them off one by one."

"But why?" questioned Bruce.

"Revenge, anger, you name it." Sylvia stared at the pitcher of the cheerleaders, and explained, "What if Paula was kicked out of the cheerleader squad, over some scandal, and had hired a killer to get even."

"Sounds plausible. But, we need to catch this killer before he strikes again."

Patrick rushed in the house, up to the woman, took out his stethoscope, checked her heart, then made a call on his cell phone saying, "I need a medevac at my position STAT! I have a young woman, with a knife in her chest clinging to life!"

Sylvia picked up the woman's leather purse, that was pushed under the couch, opened it, took out her ID and said, "Her name is Kimberly T. Stouts, and is 22 years old and weighs one hundred and thirty pounds." Sylvia took out the woman's notebook and stated, "She has written in her memos that she was to meet Police Sergeant Ben this morning before she started packing."

Bruce turned to Kim's friend, Miss Smith, and asked, "Did you happen to notice a patrol car leave her driveway this morning?"

"I did see a white van pass my house, and slow down as it turned into her driveway."

Just then, three paramedics rushed in the house, clad in light blue scrubs, carrying a red stretcher. One knelt by Kim, stabilized her, Gave Patrick the knife, and left with Kim.

Bruce turned to Martha, and warned, "Do not tell anyone that Kim is alive. Or they will be coming after you."

"I think it is time I visit my mom in Salt Lake City, Utah."

"Now would be a good time, Harry, go with her and make sure she gets off safely.

Some thirty-five minutes later, Harry returned and reported, "Miss Martha, Smith is safely off to her mother's and agreed not to stop until she was over the state line."

Sylvia suggested, "What about stopping for a nosh at the Horseshoe Cafe before we go home, I'm starved."

"I'm up for it," stated Patrick.

Inside the Cafe, Bruce stated, "The food is on me, so order what you like."

Harry and Bruce ordered a foot-long sausage and pepper grinder, with French fries, While Sylvia and Patrick ordered, roast chicken dinner with mashed potato, gravy with corn." Bruce took a bite of his hoagie when a wide-eyed young lady clad in a cranberry halter top and jeans, approached the table and frantically inquired, "Is it true that somebody is killing my friends on the old cheerleading squad?"

Bruce raised his hand and said, "Waitress, can you bring this lady a cup of coffee and whatever she wants?"

The woman pulled up a chair, sat down and said, "My name is Stacy."

The waitress gave Stacy her coffee and left, Bruce inquired, "Where did you hear about the cheerleaders being murdered?"

Stacy took a swallow of her coffee, and reported, "It's all over the news, how somebody is killing the cheerleaders and a stumble-bum of a defective that doesn't know what he is doing is handling the case."

"Don't believe everything you hear from the media. Were you one of them?"

"Yes, why?"

"My advice to you is to get in your car and leave town as soon as you can. Your life is in danger."

"Can it wait until tomorrow? You see this guy called, me today, and told me that I stand a great chance to be in the movies."

"That is the excuse the murder uses to gain access to your home. If you see him tomorrow. I promise you will be dead before the day is out."

"But, this is my chance to be famous."

"The other three thought the same thing. Now two of them are dead and one is in critical condition. Do you want to be victim number four?"

"Definitely not. I do not like being dead, thank you."

"Then get out of state now!"

"I can go to my mom in Nevada."

"One last thing. What do you know about Susan Paula Stevens? Or Paula?"

"She has kicked off the cheerleading squad for crawling in bed with the judges, so we would win the contests."

"Do you think Paula would revert to murder to get even?"

"In a heartbeat."

"Thanks, here is five hundred dollars for your trip now you better get going before you wind up dead. Harry, escort Stacy to her car."

CHAPTER 18 COMING OUT ALIVE IS THE TRICK

As they were leaving the restaurant, Bruce spotted a bunch of teenagers a stone's throw away, who seemed concern about something and stopped to asked, "Is there something wrong here?"

One kid around 19 clad in jeans, a white t-shirt, and a buzz haircut, spoke up and reported, "Some of our friends said that they were going to Old Man Snake's house to tease him. That was this morning, and we haven't heard from them since."

"Who is this Snake fella?"

"He lived on the edge of town, in an old rundown house. People go in there to talk to him, but they don't come out."

"I know the place he's talking about," stated Patrick. "I've passed by it several times and it creeps me out every time."

"What's so eerie about an abandoned house?" inquired Bruce.

"It's not the house Boss, it what's he has in the yard that makes people shutter when they walk by."

"Okay, we'll check it out. Kids buy some ice cream. And wait here, I will be back."

Forty minutes later, Bruce stopped his SUV in the yard that was overgrown with grass. Got out, and studied the various hideous looking statues of spiders, grotesques skeletons, and animals. Sylvia questioned, "Do we really have to check this place out?"

"You can stay in the car if you like."

"On second thought, I'll stay with you. How bad can it be?"

Bruce led the group to the old gray house with black shutters stepped on the porch, and stared at the upside-down welcome mat with a slight bulge in the center and said, "Stand back," picked up a rock and dropped it on the mat, triggering a trap door under the mat.

Inside, Harry pointed to a heavyset boy 18 years in an open doorway, who was clad in a blue plaid shirt and jeans at the end of the hallway, tied to a chair and gadded. Patrick cautioned, "Careful Boss, it might be a trap."

Bruce stared at the boy who was looking up at something, and said, "Sylvia, Harry stand on the right side of the door, Patrick, lay on the floor by the chair and look up and tell me what you see."

Patrick lay on his back and said, "Nothing boss. Now what?"

Bruce inched his way to the young kid in his late teens, and yanked him to one side, just as a medieval battle-ax swung down from the ceiling. Patrick hollered, "Whoa! This guy plays rough."

Sylvia untied the boy and asked, "What's your name?

"Billy Ma'am."

"Do you know where the rest of your friends are?"

"I don't know. They should be around here somewhere."

Bruce poked his head in the kitchen door to look around then said, "We're good and walked in the dingy, dusty kitchen with cabinets doors hanging by one hinge, exposing the broken dishes, laden with dust. Sylvia took hold of the pull chain to turn on the light. Bruce hollered, "Hon don't let go of the chain until I tell you. Everyone down on the floor. Bruce knelt by his wife, took hold of the top of her skirt, and said, "Now!" and pulled her down on top of him, as four spears shot across the room, and embedded in the far wall. Sylvia lay on top of her husband and whispered, "Thanks for pulling my skirt down, now everyone knows what color undies I have on."

"It was that, or have you riddled with spears."

Sylvia swallowed hard and asked, "Spears, what spears?"

"The ones sticking in the wall over there."

"Oh. Can you distract the guys for me, so, I can pull my skirt up?"

Bruce stood up, pointed to the back hall leading outside and said, "Harry, Patrick check out that hall."

Sylvia rose to her feet, trying to keep her skirt from falling any lower and whispered, "Give me a hand will ya?"

Bruce walked up to Sylvia, and inquired, "What's wrong? I like your pretty pink waistband."

"Don't get smart with me Mister, you know quite well what it is. Now help me get my skirt up before I die from embarrassment."

Bruce stood in the back of his wife, unzipped the back of her skirt, pulled it up and fastened it. Then said, "Do you know you have a hole in your undies?"

"Why don't you broadcast it to the whole world, Sylvia's underwear is full of holes!"

"Bruce took her in his arms and kissed her on the lips saying, "We'll get out of this in one piece. Trust me."

Harry approached Bruce, and reported, "You have got to see this."

Bruce cautiously walked down the dark, and dusty hall, stacked with cardboard boxes, and saw a thin 19-year-old girl dressed in blue shorts and a white top, tied in a chair suspended from the ceiling. Sylvia reassured her, "Don't worry Sweetheart we will get you out of there."

Patrick suggested, "I think the girl's weight is a counterbalance. We take her out of that chair and something is gonna come crashing through the wall at us."

"Are you sure?" questioned Bruce.

"Yes, look at the way the rope is tied to the ceiling."

"Any suggestions?" asked Bruce.

"I'll slide under the chair, hold the bottom rung of the chair, and keep the rope tight, while you free the girl. But how are you going to get her free?"

"I haven't thought that far yet." Bruce slowly untied the girl, asking, "What's your name?"

"Sherrie, cried the girl trying to hold back the tears."

"Okay, this is what we are going to do." stated Bruce, "Carefully put your arms around my neck and slide off the seat a little at a time." Bruce stated, "Alright Patrick here we go."

Once the girl was off the chair, Harry opened the back door, and let everyone out. Bruce took hold of Patrick's feet and instructed, "When I tell you, let go of the chair. Do it."

"You got it, Boss."

Bruce hollered, "Now!" Bruce and Patrick tumbled backward out the door as a giant boulder crashed through the wall and smashed the chair."

Patrick sprang to his feet and stated, "Next time try being a little faster. Another second slower and my head would have been under that boulder."

Sylvia pointed to a white shed and asked, "Shall we check that place next?"

Bruce turned to his wife and instructed, "Stay here with Patrick and the children. Harry and I are going to search the cellar first."

Harry opened the basement hatchway and descended stating, "I think half the spiders in Arizona are right here in this guy's cellar."

Bruce followed Harry down the stairs into the basement crowded with old furniture, toilet, and car parts. He brushed the cobwebs out of his face, and saw a half dozen black harry spiders scurry across the basement floor, and commented, "I see what you mean."

Harry held up his hand then pointed to his left. Bruce circled in the opposite direction to see a four-foot man make a mad dash for the open basement door. Bruce dove forward and tackled the man but could not hold him. Harry leveled his Winchester at the fleeing man and shot him in his right thigh. He struggled to his feet and Harry shot him in his left leg, and warned, "One more move Mister, and I'll splatter your brains all over creation."

Bruce grabbed the guy's right arm and Harry took the other and they dragged him outside and dropped him on the ground. Bruce stated, forcefully, "You reek little man! When was the last time you took a shower?"

"That's none of your business. Now get me to a doctor before I bleed to death."

"Not until you tell me why you kidnapped these kids."

"They were trespassing on my property so I dealt with the matter."

Billy shouted, "I heard you tell someone called, Ben that you would take care of the matter."

"That wouldn't happen to be Sergeant Ben, would it?"

The man's eyes darted about as he tried to find the words to reply. Harry jammed his rifle in his chest and ordered, "Answer him!"

"Go ahead and kill me. I am as good as dead anyway."

Bruce ordered, "Patrick, Call Duncan so he can get this thing out of my sight."

Bruce walked to an old shed, shot off the lock with his 44 Magnum, pushed open the door to find metal shavings turned over oil cans and tools scattered everywhere. Harry approached a 12-foot-long pipe and asked, "Look familiar?"

Sylvia picked up a thin knife off the floor and stated, "I think what's his name has been making the cannons for the killer."

"Let's just call him B.O. Plenty" stated Harry.

"It sure fits." muttered Bruce."

Patrick entered the shed and reported, "Duncan's men are here. Is there anything else you want them to do?"

"Yes. I need them to catalog the stuff in here." Bruce brushed some metal junk off the bench and spotted Police Sergeant Ben's Business card and a hand-written note that read, "I need 17 knives that will shoot out of cannons. Sergeant Ben Backwater. Bruce held up the note and stated, "We are going to see the Sarge."

Sylvia tapped her husband's shoulder and reminded him, "Aren't you supposed to meet the children back at the ice cream place?"

"Oh yeah, I forgot about that."

Three men dressed in gray suits entered the shed, walked up to Bruce, one of them stated, "We have the prisoner in custody. Is there anything else you need?"

"Yes. The prisoner has been making the cannons and the thin knives for the killer. All the stuff in here should be cataloged."

"Yes, Sir. We'll get on it right away Sir."

Bruce hollered, "Okay everybody, in the SUV! It's time for Ice cream!"

Back at the ranch, Harry and Stubs went home for the day, Alexis and Patrick retired to their room, for some quality time. Sylvia brought her husband out to the barn, closed the doors, and locked them. Bruce inquired with a puzzled look on his face, "What's up Sweet?"

Sylvia snuggled close to Bruce, and said, "I've been wanting you all day."

"Going commando again I see."

"I wanted to be ready when we came home."

"I thought you didn't like romping in the hay?"

"I changed my mind. Out here, there is no phone to bother us, no one can pound on our door. It's just you and me. Now, let's go up in the hayloft, and have some fun."

Two hours later, Bruce rolled over, kissed his wife, and asked, "You want to make some coffee, and set on the front porch?"

"How about we relax in the gazebo outback? We'll have more privacy there."

Halfway to the house, Bruce glanced at his wife, and inquired, "What's wrong? Why are you walking funny?"

"That hay made my skin itch."

In the house, Sylvia made a mad dash for the shower hollering, "You make the coffee, while I shower!"

Sometime later, sitting in the gazebo, Sylvia was drinking her tea, relaxing in her, long pink nightgown with Bruce. When Flash their cat scampered on the gazebo, jumped on her lap, and dug his claws in her leg. Sylvia cried, "Hey, easy with the claws will 'ya!"

"What's up with Flash?" question Bruce.

"I don't know. But, he's sure nervous about something. He's probably looking for attention."

Bruce lifted his head, and muttered, "We better head for the house it's gonna rain."

"Right behind you Sweet." Partway to the house, the sky opened up and dropped a deluge of rain. Sylvia walked in the back-door grumbling, "Couldn't the rain at least wait until we were in the house. No, it had to make sure that we looked like drowned rats." Sylvia glared at her husband and snapped, "What are you smiling about?"

"You look great in a wet nightgown, you know that."

"I'm going to bed. So, goodnight!"

"Make sure you put on a dry nightie."

"Who needs a nightgown?"

Just then, a loud clap of thunder shook the house, Sylvia ran out of the bedroom screaming and into her husband's arms trembling. Bruce muttered, "I hope it didn't hit one of my wind turbines."

Sylvia looked in her husband's eyes, and asked, softly, "Why don't you come to bed, and keep me company."

CHAPTER 19 A CAGE RATTLING EVENT

Early the next morning, Sylvia woke reached for her husband, and found that he wasn't there, but found a note that read. You looked so peaceful sleeping; I didn't want to wake you. I found our clothed in the barn and put them in the wash. I went to check on the wind turbines, see you at lunch. Hubby."

Sylvia put on her long, blue cotton bathrobe, went out into the kitchen, and made herself a bacon, egg, and cheese sandwich, poured herself a mug of coffee and walked to the gazebo to enjoy her breakfast. Two feet from the gazebo, Police Sergeant Ben, stepped out, pointed his gun at her and said, "I hear you, and your husband was snooping around the Morrison place yesterday."

"Who?" questioned Sylvia.

"You know, the old house with the weird things on the front lawn."

"Yeah, so what's it to you?"

"Stay away from Chris Morrison. He's an old man and has nothing to do with the murders." He then put his gun to Sylvia's chest.

Sylvia threw her hot coffee in his face, and kicked him between his pockets, sending him to the ground in pain. Before she had a chance to run, the Sergeant grabbed Sylvia's right leg, causing her to tumble to the ground. The Sergeant rolled over, sat on her hip, and said, "Mrs. Birdson, you are going to be the killer's next victim. Took out a long thin knife, slowly ran the point down the center of her chest to her belly button, saying "I really hate to do this to you, but, your husband doesn't leave me any choice. However, if your husband sells this ranch to my boss the killings will stop."

"Get off of me!" shouted Sylvia, and tried knocking the Sergeant off her. He stuck his knife under her chin and ordered, "Lay still, and don't make a sound," then belted her on the jaw, knocking her out.

Sylvia woke an hour later, laying on top of her bed, with one of her thin nightgowns next to her. Patrick popped his head in the front screen door and hollered, "Anybody home?"

Sylvia hollered, mournfully, "I'm in the bedroom."

Patrick entered the bedroom, saw Sylvia, and said, "I am so sorry for barging in on you Mrs. Sylvia."

Sylvia wrapped herself in the bedsheet and said, "That's alright. You didn't know."

"What's troubling you, ma'am? If you don't mind me asking you?"

"I had an encounter with Sergeant Ben by the gazebo and he told me that I was going to be The killer's next victim. I woke on my bed later still alive."

"I'll get me medical bag and check you out."

Patrick returned eleven minutes later, and asked, "Sylvia, can you get on the bed and lay on your back?"

Twenty-two minutes later, Patrick approached Sylvia dressed in brown slacks and a yellow top sitting on the front porch, drinking her herbal tea, and reported, "I have the results. You are clean. I didn't pick up any foreign DNA, and there was no sign of a forced entry. I also checked you for any kind of lubricant, and there was none."

"Are you sure?"

"Positive. I also downloaded Ben's medical file and found out that he had an accident last year that left him on the wimpy side if you know what I mean."

"Then why did he put me on my bed?"

"I noticed a negligee laying on the bed next to you when I barged in. Were you planning to wear it?"

"No, I don't know how that got there and it is not mine."

"The Sergeant was getting you ready to kill you and must have been interrupted by someone."

"Most likely it was Flash our cat. He'll attack anyone who tries to hurt me."

"Oh, I found this computer card on your bedroom floor. You must have lost it out of your camera."

Sylvia looked at it and stated, "That didn't come from my camera. Let's see what's on it." She inserted the chip in her computer and brought up fifty images of women and grumbled, "Pervert,"

The pictures were of murdered victims clad in skimpy attire, being stabbed by an unknown assailant who wore black leather gloves. Sylvia shouted, "Patrick! Come here. I have something to show you!"

Patrick and Alexis entered the den, Patrick questioned, "What is it?"

"This computer chip has photos of each victim being murdered from every angle. Look. Here is a photo of Sasha C. Dixon laying on the floor in a blue slack suit with a knife in her chest."

Patrick stated, "But when Bruce found her she was wearing just a white negligee, and there was no sign of those clothes anywhere."

Sylvia moved to the next photo and stated, "That's Miss Kimberly T. Stouts, but in this picture, she is fully dressed, but when we found her she was wearing pink intimate apparel."

"It sounds like we have a sick killer on our hands if you ask me," stated Alexis.

Bruce walked up behind his wife, gave her a peck on the cheek, and said, "Sorry I'm late, wind turbine fifty was struck by lightning, and for some reason melted one of the blades."

"What do you want for lunch, Hon?"

"We need to grab a few sandwiches, drinks and head out, Kimberly Stouts is awake, and wants to talk to the police."

"Are you coming, Patrick?"

"No, I'll stay here with me wife."

Bruce's eye caught the images on the computer screen and inquired, "Where did you get those from?"

Sergeant Ben dropped in when he tried to kill me this morning. Thanks to Flash he didn't."

"I want to look at those when we get back."

Sylvia threw a lunch together, followed her husband out the door, and jumped in the front seat of the SUV. Harry quickly hopped in the backseat and stated, "I'm going with you just in case you meet up with trouble."

Bruce entered the hospital room and inquired, "Miss Kimberly T. Stouts?"

"Yes. Who are you?"

"I am Marshal Bruce Birdson. The one who found you. This is my wife Sylvia, and my good friend Harry. Is it alright if I ask you some questions?"

"Sure. Ask me anything except my age." quipped Kim.

"Do you know who stabbed you?"

"It was Police Sergeant Ben. He called me two days ago and told me that he had connections to Hollywood, and would I be interested in a photoshoot.

I told him sure. He drove up in a white van and rang my doorbell. I let him in, and we discussed the pictures he wanted to take of me. When I agreed, Sergeant, Ben brought in his equipment along with a brown bag full of something. I watched him set up his camera. Then he told me to stand on the black, bearskin rug by the fireplace, for the first picture. He looked at me and said, "Something is not right, walked up to me stared me in the eye then struck me in the chest with his fist knocking me down. Before I had a chance to scream for help, he kicked me several times. The last thing I remember is Sergeant Ben bending over me with a knife."

"Do you go to Pastor Giles's church?"

"Yes. I gave my life to Christ there. Why do you ask?"

"Then why did you pose in a thin pink negligee? When you knew better."

"I don't even own one of those things. I had on my yellow sundress. Why?"

"That's what you were wearing when I found you."

"That Creep took off my clothes after he knocked me out!"

"Miss Stouts. How many of you were on the Cheerleading squad?"

"Sorry for my anger, 17 counting myself."

"I understand. What do you know about a woman by the name of Susan Paula Stevens?"

"I was told that she was kicked off the squad for sleeping with the contest judges."

"What do you know about a man about six feet tall, thin gaunt face, light brown hair that looks like he was caught in a windstorm?"

"Yeah, That's Paula's so-called boyfriend and partner in crime in all her scams."

"Can you expound on that?"

"During a road trip, Paula fell and hurt her foot, sued the place and got a large out of court settlement. I know she didn't injure herself because I saw her a few days later walking around without a limp. When I tried to report it. She made me look like a liar."

"Why would Paula have her boyfriend pose as the killer?"

"To throw the police off the trail of the real killer."

"Then Sergeant Ben and Paula are lovers."

"In every sense of the word, until she kicked him where it hurt him the most. But he keeps coming back to her. That last time I heard they might get married."

"Do you think someone paid Paula to hired Sergeant Ben to kill everyone on the cheerleader squad?"

"Definitely."

A medium-built man in his thirties walked in the room holding a long white box, stared at Kim and said, "I have a delivery for Kim." Harry grabbed Kimberly, and Sylvia pulled her on the floor, as he took out a semi-automatic out of the box and riddled the room with bullets. Bruce fell to the floor, and fired his 44 Magnum, striking the assailant in the chest, killing him."

The Hospital security rushed in the room to find out what was happening. Bruce reported, "That man just tried to kill Kim. It was only by God's grace that no one was killed. My suggestion is, contact Duncan and have his men take Miss Stouts to an undefined location until Sergeant Ben is caught."

"Sound like a good idea, Sir."

Bruce kissed Kimberly on her cheek, and said, "Don't worry, Duncan's men will take good care of you." he then dropped his wife off at a nearby restaurant, then entered the Police station with Harry and demanded to see Police Sergeant, Ben, then barged into his office.

Ben leaned back in his chair, and inquired, "Gentleman. What's on your mind?"

"You are under arrest for the murder of Sasha C. Dixon, Miss Star Bower, and the tempt murder of, Kimberly T. Stouts," stated Bruce.

"That's a bold statement. Do you have any proof to back that up? If not. Get out of my office before I have you two thrown in jail."

"Kimberly is awake and talking. Oh, I hate to inform you but the one you sent to kill her is dead, and Miss Stouts is somewhere where you can't find her. Oh, then there is Miss Paula, who is tucked away somewhere. Are you coming along quietly or, do I have to drag you?"

Sergeant Ben, rose to his feet, walked around his desk, quickly pulled out a taser and shot Bruce, then landed a right cross to Harry's jaw, and sprinted out the office hollering, "Arrest those men! They just tried to kill me!" He then escaped.

The officer's in the police station mobbed Bruce and Harry beat them severely before throwing them in the lockup to await their trial. Three hours later, they were told it was all a big misunderstanding and were released.

Back at the ranch, Bruce asked, "Patrick, wake up Paula. I need to speak to her about Sergeant Ben."

Patrick helped Paula to sit on the edge of her bed wearing a red nightie and gave her a drink of water. Bruce questioned, "Paula, I know you hired the police Sergeant to wipe out the old cheerleading squad. Where is he?"

"What are you talking about? Yes, I was furious when they kicked me off the team, but I didn't hire Ben to kill them."

"Then who hired Ben to kill the cheerleaders?"

"I don't know!" screamed Paula.

"Didn't you have an affair with him?"

"No. Ben would come to my place and pay me to strut around in my undies. It was good money. But, I didn't want to get in bed with him.

"Then, who wants the cheerleaders dead?"

"Ben coached the squad before he became police Sergeant. That's all I know." Paula paused for a bit, then stated, "The girls on the squad, gave Ben the heave-ho because they didn't like the way he barged in the locker room when they were changing. The squad then hired Maze Greentree, who whipped us into shape, and we began to win trophies. That's when I was thrown off the squad."

"Why did you and your boyfriend stage a fake attempt of murder?"

Paula hung her head and confessed, "Sergeant Ben hired me to find a way to seduce you so you were in your wife would split up. With you and your wife divorced your ranch would be up for grabs and the man that hired Tucker and Sergeant Ben to force you off your land would have it. Now, if you will excuse me, I need some fresh air."

"Who hired Tucker and Ben?"

Paula ignored Bruce, walked outside and sat down at a table under the shelter in the cool night air, saw Patrick and asked, "Could you get me something cold to drink?" She then suddenly fell backward with a bullet in her chest. Bruce pulled his pistol and scanned the darkness but could not see anyone. Patrick called 911 on his cell phone saying, "I have a white female about one hundred and forty pounds with an bullet in her chest. Her pulse and breathing are shallow."

CHAPTER

20 THE NIGHT VISITOR

With Paula safely on her way to the hospital, Bruce sat on the front porch with his wife and inquired, "Sweet, I'm at a loss. Do you have any idea as to who shot Paula?"

"Paula knows who is the one trying to squeeze you off your land and she was shot to keep silent. However, Maze Greentree, and the cheerleaders fits into this somehow. This is just hypothetically speaking. what if Miss Greentree took out an insurance policy on the cheerleaders. Later on, she fell into financial trouble and decided to cash in on the policy, by killing off the cheerleaders and is trying to put the blame on you so you will give up your ranch because of disgrace."

"That sounds plausible. But, we have to prove it."

Sylvia stared at her husband and asked, "Hello, husband of mine. You want to come back to reality."

"Sorry, I was wondering how we are going to catch Sergeant Ben."

"Why don't you put Stubs on that. Now, enough of business for tonight. I'll put a pot of coffee on and open a box of soft oatmeal and raison cookies."

Later, Bruce took a bite of his cookie, and asked, "If Maze is indeed the one who hired the killer. We have to connect her with Sergeant Ben. I still say Paula is the one behind the killings not Maze Greentree."

"Let's look her up first thing tomorrow and pay her a visit. Hey, how are the wind turbines doing?"

"One wind generator was fried when lightning struck it, but, all in all, their doing pretty good."

Sylvia crawled out of bed the next morning, walked out in the kitchen in her yellow nightshirt to make some tea for herself, and coffee for Bruce, and collapsed on the floor. She opened her eyes to see Barbra slapping her face saying, "Come on Sylvia open those eyes of your." She sat up looked around and asked, "What am I doing outside like this? And where is my husband?"

"I found you passed out on the kitchen floor, and your husband asleep in bed. It seems someone was trying to suffocate you two with gas. The only thing that saved you two is that you had your bedroom window open."

Sylvia glanced at her husband lying on the grass in his PJ bottoms, then at Barbra, and suggested, "Barb, why don't you start cleaning in the back bedroom today." When Barbra was gone, Sylvia asked, "Hon. Did she get friendly with you?"

"Don't worry about that. Let's get breakfast and pay a visit to Maze Greentree."

"Hey, I'm just protecting what's mine. Did you and her get into it while I was passed out?"

"No, so stop worrying,"

Sylvia followed her husband in the house trying to prevent Barbra from seeing too much of her husband's bare chest.

After breakfast, Bruce and Sylvia drove west on Route 60 to west Palo Verde Drive. A stately woman in her mid-fifties answered the door and asked, "Can I help you Sir?"

"Maze Greentree. I'm Marshal Bruce Birdson and this is my partner, and wife Sylvia, I would like to ask you a few questions about the cheerleaders."

"Would you like something cold to drink?"

"Yes, thank you."

The woman handed Bruce and his wife their drinks, and stated, "Fire away Marshal."

"What do you know about a Miss Susan Paula Stevens?"

"She was a great cheerleader, but, I had to let her go because of her immoral actions."

"I understand you took out quite a large insurance policy on the team that would pay you three million dollars if anything happened to them. Can you tell me why that policy was never canceled?"

"I had to protect my investments, and what's it to you whether that policy was canceled or not."

"The squad became quite a lucrative investment for you and put you on easy street you might say. But, how much of that money did the team see?"

"They got their share."

"I've been going over your financial records Miss Greentree, and you owe a lot of money."

"I think it's time for you to leave, Marshal."

"Do you know a Police Sergeant Ben Backwaters"

"No, now, get out of my house!"

On their way back home, Bruce asked, "Do you think she is hiding something?"

"Oh yeah. When she went to get us something to drink, I stuffed her phone bill in my purse."

"What does it say?"

"Give me a minute. Look here, someone called her three times by the name of Benjamin, Willis. Let's see who it is." Sylvia dialed the number, and a voice answered, "Sergeant Ben speaking. Can I help you?"

Sylvia replied in a high squeaky voice, "Sorry, wrong number." then hung up. She then shouted, "BINGO! It's our old friend Ben of the police department."

"I think Paula had a hand in this somewhere."

Just then, a dark gray, pickup rammed the back of their SUV, pulled on the left side of the vehicle and tried to run them off the road. Bruce stated, "Hold on, to your bloomers." Then hit the super charger, injecting Nitrous oxide into the engine, putting plenty of distance between him and the pickup. Sylvia turned around to see if the pickup was still behind then and inquired, "What was that all about?"

"I think we struck a nerve with Miss Greentree. Do you want to stop for a nosh?"

"What about that restaurant on North Tegner street?"

"That will work."

In the parking lot of the restaurant, Sylvia pointed to a woman unable to get out of her parking spot because of a green car parked right behind her, and said, "Hon, do you think you could help the poor woman?"

Bruce stepped out of his vehicle and approached the middle-aged woman's car and asked, "Is there anything I can do?"

"Yes. Some young kid parked in back of me when I was backing out. I had asked him if he could move but he refused."

Bruce noticed that the car was from Connecticut. Walked in the restaurant and asked the woman at the cashier if she knew who owned the green car from Connecticut. A young man turned around and said, "That's my car. Why?"

"You are blocking a woman. can you please move it?"

"I will when I get my order."

"No. you will do it now."

"Mister, I said that I will move my car when I am good and ready. Now, back off before I give you a fat lip."

Bruce snatched the small plastic bag from his side pocket, and stated forcefully, "You will move your car, now. Or go to jail for having a controlled substance in your possession. Oh, I forgot to tell you I'm, Marshal Bruce Birdson. Now, move your car!"

The young man stormed out, got in his car, stepped on the gas, and pealed out as he sped out of the parking lot, and broadsided a police car.

A short time later, Bruce pulled his SUV in the lumberyard on East Yavapai Street, Wickenburg, Arizona. Sylvia stared at a woman in her mid-thirties hobbling up the street with a cane and set on the bench across from her. Sylvia jumped out of the vehicle saying, "Bruce, I'll be on the bench across the street." Sylvia sat next to the woman and asked, "Mandy Prince is that really you?"

"Sylvia! What on Earth are you doing in this part of the world? I haven't seen you since I was18."

"Mandy, you used to be such a happy go lucky gal. Now you look like you have the weight of the world on your shoulders. What's wrong?"

"I'm fine." stated Mandy solemnly.

"No, you're not, Mandy. We were best bud from when we were in diapers and we never held secrets from each other. When you reached 18, you started to act quiet and gloomy as if something was troubling you. I tried to get you to tell me, but, you told me to leave you alone. So, I did. Now, woman to woman. What's wrong?"

"I can't tell you."

"You're still my best buds. Hey, remember the prank we pulled on your cousin Carl at your 18th birthday party?"

Mandy remained silent as tears streamed down her face. Sylvia gazed at her friend and inquired sharply, "What did Carl do to you?"

Mandy explained sobbing, "As you know I sleep with a nightshirt on. Anyways after Carl finished molesting me in my room, he got in my face and threatened me physical harm if I told my folks."

"Couldn't you have done something to stop him, like tell your parents?" questioned a concerned Sylvia.

Mandy hollered, "I tried to but, I was told I was lying, he was the family's idle, that couldn't do anything wrong. I tried to resist a few more times but Carl broke three of my ribs. When I turned 20, I moved out of town to get away from him. Oh, I had a few boyfriends but, they didn't last, because I would have flash back of Carl, every time my boyfriend kissed me."

Mandy lowered her head for a moment, then jerked it up and screamed, "It was my fault for letting him in my room in the first place!"

"It wasn't your fault Mandy. So, stop blaming yourself. By the way. How many people have you told this to?"

"No one, so please do not tell a soul what Carl did to me twenty years ago."

Sylvia took hold of Mandy's shoulders, looked her in the eyes and stated firmly, "You have to speak up. This thing has been inside of you for twenty years destroying you little by little. You let Carl rob you of your peace of mind, self-respect, your health. If you keep it locked up inside of you, it will eventually kill you."

"It's my life, so, don't go telling me what to do!" snapped Mandy.

"Look at you. You're 38 years old and can hardly walk you are so crippled up."

Mandy insisted, "I am fine! So just go away!"

"No Mandy, I will not let you do this to yourself. Where do you live? I'll have my husband drive you to your place so, I can help you pack. Because you are staying with me and Bruce."

"I don't want to put you out."

"We have more room than we know what to do with."

Mandy suddenly tensed up, as Sergeant Ben walked up clad in jeans and a t-shirt, placed his hand on the small of her back and said, "I missed you last night. Hey, I know, let's get together tonight. I know we will have lodes of fun."

Gusty Sylvia, stood up, stuck her finger in Ben's face and stated, "Back off Creep if you know what's good for you."

Ben grabbed Sylvia around her waist, placed his hand on her thigh, and said, "I see you need to learn a few lessons. How about giving Ben, a squeeze?"

Bruce walked up behind Ben, tapped him on the shoulder and said, "Take your hands off my wife."

"Well look who we have here. I suppose you are going to give me a pounding. Yeah, like that gonna happen. Not!"

Bruce clenched his fist and cold cocked Ben, sending to the ground out cold. Mandy stared down at Ben, threw her arms around Bruce, and gave him a friendly squeeze.

Bruce inquired, "How did you get mixed up with Sergeant Ben Backwaters?"

"My friend Sasha Dixon told me that she was going to be in the movies and if I talked to Ben I might get a break."

Mr. Backwaters is wanted for murdering your friend Sasha. So why don't you get in my SUV and you can stay at my ranch until the investigation is over."

In the SUV, Sylvia stated, "Hon, can you drop by The Rancho Vista Apartment on West Penn Lane? I want to help Mandy pack."

"Sure, we should be there in ten minutes."

Back at the ranch, Harry greeted them saying, "Boss, number 15 wind-turbine, needs maintenance and you got the lab report on cigarette butt you found, it was definitely Sergeant Ben's."

Mandy got out of the SUV, smiled at Harry and asked, "Could you please help me with my things?"

"Yes, ma'am. Where are you staying?"

Sylvia suggested, "Mandy, you can stay in the house, or take one of the rooms in the bunkhouse."

"If there are no guys staying there, I'll take the bunkhouse."

"Breakfast is at nine, lunch is at noon and supper is at five, stated Sylvia.

Harry put the last of Mandy's things in her room and stated, "Don't worry miss, you will be safe here."

"Why do you say that? No one is after me."

"Somebody hurt you really bad; because I can see the hurt etched on your face. Besides you don't know Sergeant Ben."

"I will be fine, now if you will excuse me, I have to put away my clothes."

Harry smiled, took her by the hand saying, "If anyone tries to harm you in any way. Just tell me and I'll fix their wagon."

Mandy stared at her hand in Harry's and said softly, "Don't do that."

"All I am doing is holding your hand." Harry smiled, let go and was about to leave when Mandy said, "Can I talk to you Sir?"

CHAPTER 21 GREENTREE

The next morning, Harry was dressed and sat at the picnic table under the shelter reading his New Testament trying to figure out why he blew it with Mandy last night. Bruce walked up, sat across from him, and stated, "You look lower than a snake's belly in a wagon rut. What happened? You and Mandy get into things last night?"

"Something like that. I heard a noise coming from Mandy's room, went to investigate and I found Carl in her room. Once I took care of Carl, I wound up sleeping with Mandy."

"Harry, you are human, and you haven't been out on a date with a woman since Sally died. When you saw Mandy's lovely curves, the passion you felt for her took over and you indulged yourselves."

"Dang it all, Bruce, I'm a Christian."

"You and Mandy are meant for each other. The Lord has provided your forgiveness through the cross. Repent of your sin and go on in Christ. Breakfast is on the table."

"Thanks for the talk, I'll get Mandy."

At the breakfast table, Harry pulled out a chair for Mandy clad in a bright yellow blue, then sat next to her. Mandy rubbed Harry's right arm asked, "Do you know how much I love you?"

Harry pulled his arm away and kept on eating his apple pancakes. Sylvia glanced at her husband but said nothing. After breakfast, Harry put his plate in the sink, and said, "Bruce, I'm going into town to pick up some supplies.

Sylvia quickly replied, "Harry. Could you order me some red bark mulch for my flowerbed?"

"Sure, Gotta go." and rushed out the door.

Sylvia stared at Mandy and inquired, "Okay, out with it. Yesterday you were Miss Glum, today you're smiling like a Cheshire cat. Is there something you are not telling me?" Sylvia poured coffee in a stainless-steel pot, placed some pastries on a platter and said, "Let's sit on the front porch so we can talk."

Mandy sat in a cedar chair, took a bite of her pastry and said, "Late last night Carl paid me a visit, but before he could do anything, Harry stopped him. I was so thankful that Harry came To my rescue. I used my feminine charm on him. But I wanted to give Harry something, so I gave him me. But, now he won't talk to me. Did I do something to hurt him?"

Harry gave his life to Christ when he was a small boy and has never been with a woman since his wife died. So, by you doing what you did with him hurt Harry really bad."

"Will he be alright?"

"Mandy, you have heard many times that Christ died on the Cross to wash away your sins with His blood. Would you like to ask Christ into your heart and to forgive you of your sins and cleanse you from all unrighteousness?"

"I guess I have nothing to lose."

Right after Mandy gave her life to Christ, she smiled and said, "Wow. I feel clean inside. Thank you. But now I have to Confess. Sergeant Ben paid me $10,000 to seduce Harry."

"Can I ask you why?"

"With Harry out of the way, Ben was going to take out Bruce, then why you are grieving over the loss of your husband he would manipulate the ranch away from you. I am so sorry that i used our friendship. Now, if you excuse me I will pack and hitchhike back to Wickenburg."

"You will do no such thing. We're best buds and friends don't bail just because the other one messed up."

With Mandy gone back to her room, Sylvia gave her husband a hug, and said, "You sit here while I make us a nice dessert." Sylvia came out ten minutes later dressed in a coral pink negligee, handed Bruce his coffee, and a slice of apple pie. Saw the grin on her husband's face and remarked, "No, I am not on the menu, but, we can get into things, later. What's bugging you?"

"Paula is what's bugging me. Why would someone stage an attack that would almost kill them?"

"Sergeant Ben gave Paula a lot of money to seduce you and break up our marriage. Then Ben would grad the ranch and make a lot of money by selling it to the one who's been trying to force you off your ranch."

"Then why was Paula's so-called boyfriend trying to kill her if it wasn't staged?"

"Simple, Paula failed so her boyfriend was hired to get rid of her so there wouldn't be anyone that would point the finger at him." Sylvia spotted a car coming up the dusty road and darted in the house to put something on. Bruce greeted, "Pastor Giles. What brings you out at this time of the night?"

"You passed by me this afternoon like a bat out of, well. you know, and I figured that it was time to tell you."

Sylvia came out on the porch clad in a burgundy sun dress, gave the Pastor a cup of coffee and a slice of pie. Pastor Giles went on to say: Sasha C. Dixon, Miss Star Bower, and Kimberly T. Stouts all gave their life to Christ six months ago. All of them came in my office later and confessed that, while they were in the cheerleader squad, they were smuggling drugs for Miss, Maze Greentree. When the drugs were confiscated. Sergeant Ben would give them to Paula, who would give them to Miss Greentree. She would give them to her girls who would get the money and give it to Miss Greentree. After the cheerleaders broke up the girls still smuggled drugs up until they got saved. That's when Maze Greentree put a hit out on them."

"I talked to Kimberly and she didn't say a word about her involvement in drugs."

"None of them will. I'm the only one they confessed to. Oh, Paula's boyfriend was found this morning out in the desert beaten to death."

"There is a missing piece to this mystery. Because someone keeps taking out people that have tried to get this ranch from me and it started around the same time miss Greentree put a hit out on the cheerleaders. which means Ben, Greentree, Paula, her boyfriend and Tucker are all connected to someone But who that is I don't know just yet."

The pastor smiled and said, "I guess you could call this the Wickenburg Mystery because everyone involved in this is from Wickenburg, Arizona."

"Thank you, Pastor, all I have to do is prove Mess Greentree is selling drugs.

"I almost forgot. Paula called me today and gave her life to Christ."

"Do you think she would wear a wire for me, so I can get some evidence on, Miss Greentree?"

"Paula is still in serious condition in the hospital but I know someone by the name of Dug, who might be interested in. He has a black belt and wants to help."

"Great, tell him that I will meet him at the north end of Palm Lake trail tomorrow afternoon at 2:00. I'll be the one wearing the red t-shirt."

The Pastor shook Bruce's hand saying, "I pray that I have given you some information that will capture the one behind that's trying to steal your ranch. I'll see you and your wife in Church Sunday.

That evening, Sylvia slipped into her coral pink negligee, sat next to her husband In the porch and inquired, "Do you think Miss Greentree had someone try to have us run off the road?"

"I got his plate number and I'll do a check on him tomorrow. You want to come along tomorrow when I meet Dug?"

"What I want to do is turn out all the lights cuddle up to you and look at the stars."

"Sounds good to me."

Some five minutes later, Bruce whispered, "I think I heard someone coming."

Suddenly a light shone in their faced and a voice stated, "My, don't you look nice ma'am. Sorry, the Boss wants you two out of the way." before he could pull the trigger, Sylvia used her feminine charm to distract him and asked, "You wouldn't shoot me, would you?"

The shooter shone his flashlight on Sylvia, as he stepped closer to get a better look. Sylvia forced a smile, doubled up her fist, and landed a hard blow between his pockets, sending him down on the porch groaning. Bruce quickly kicked the gun out of his hands, hauled him to his feet, and handcuffed him. Sylvia went in to change and wait for Duncan's men to arrive. Bruce turned to the gunman and questioned, "Do you have a name?"

"It's Kasey."

"Where is your bow, and arrow?"

"What are you talking about? I hate those things."

"Then you didn't shoot Paula?"

"No. Ben sent me here to take you two out Then Mandy."

"Why Mandy?"

"She knows too much."

Once Kasey was hauled off, Bruce hollered, "Sylvia? Where are you?"

All he heard was silence, he went out to the gazebo and there was Sylvia, sitting down wearing a long flannel nightgown looking forlorn."

Bruce sat next to her and asked, "What's up sexy?"

"Nothing, just leave me alone!" snapped Sylvia.

"Okay, out with it."

"I don't know, what possessed me to give that gunman a peek before I covered myself."

"By doing that, you saved our lives. Now, let's go to bed."

At the north end of Palm Lake trail the next morning. Dug, a well-built man, six feet four with short hair walked up to Bruce and said, "Hi, I'm Dug. You have something for me?"

"I want you to wear this good luck charm around your neck. In it has a listening device, and my man Stubs will be on the other end, if you kneed backup."

"You want me to get enough evidence on Miss Greentree, so you can put her away for good."

"Do you think you can do it?"

"I know exactly what to do, Sir. I want the one who killed my Kimberly taken down."

"Are you talking about Kimberly T. Stouts?"

"Yes, I was planning to ask her to marry me."

"Just between you and me, Miss Stouts is alive, but we have to keep her hidden until this is all over. So, meet me here in three days, and whatever you do, don't say a word about Miss Stouts, the Lord watch over you."

In Bruce's SUV, he stated, "I forgot to tell you Hon. We are going to arrest Sergeant Ben. Harry will be waiting for us outside police headquarters."

Some two hours later outside the police station, Harry greeted Bruce, handed him the arrest warrant, and said, "Let's go."

Bruce stopped Harry and said, "Ben's gonna have friends who will warn him. Why don't you go to the impound lot, just in case he makes a break for it?"

Inside the police station, Bruce walked up to the desk and stated, "I need to see Police Sergeant Ben Backwaters."

"He is busy right now. Do you want to leave a message?"

"No. I'm Marshal Bruce Birdson and I am here to arrest him for the murder of, Sasha C. Dixon, Miss Star Bower, and the tempt murder of, Kimberly T. Stouts."

The desk clerk replied in astonishment, "You have got to be kidding? The Sergeant would never do anything like that."

Bruce unholstered his 44 Magnum and said, "Who do you think was stealing those drugs from the police lockup? They just didn't walk out on their own."

A crash echoed through the police station and Bruce rushed outside into the impound lot, to find Sergeant Ben's car smashed into a camper and gone. Harry walked up to Bruce and reported, "Sorry Sir. He got away."

A dozen police officers rushed on the scene, leveled their guns on them and shouted, "Freeze!"

Bruce raised his hands and said, "If you will open the trunk of Sergeant Ben's car, you will find some of the missing drugs, and the kind of knives that killed those cheerleaders. I only ask one thing. Keep it a secret until after I capture the brains behind this."

When they opened the trunk of the car, they found twenty kilos of marijuana, fifty kilos of cocaine, plus dried blood stains on the trunk carpeting. The acting Sergeant stated, "Okay you have three days to catch the one behind this drug kingpin and bring her to justice."

Back at Palm Lake, Bruce pointed to a large tree and suggested that they sit and relax. Then suggested, "Let's sit and talk about things that doesn't pertain to the Silent Killer case."

"Hey, can we go camping after this case is over?" question Silvia.

"Sure, as long as you don't Get lost in the desert the way you did last time."

"Who, me? Show my bare derriere in public? Never."

"Do you mind if we camp in the same place?"

"No. as long as we don't get burned out the way we did last time."

Three days later, Dug handed Bruce the surveillance tape and reported, "We have her dead to rights."

"What's the game plan?"

"Miss Greentree thinks the police Sergeant has been taken down, and she told me to meet her tomorrow in front of the lumberyard at eight AM and take her car with the shipment of cocaine to Texas."

"Perfect. Meet her, and take the drugs, that's when I'll spring the trap."

The next morning, in front of the lumberyard, Dug was leaning against the building when a dark blue 2019 Lexus stopped in front of him and Miss Greentree stepped out clad in a broad brimmed straw hat, and white slacks and a top, with two bodyguards. Dug approached her, and asked, "Can I help you ma'am?"

She opened her trunk, showed Dug the thirty kilos a cocaine and stated, "I need you to take this to Amerelow, Texas. The address is logged in the car's GPS, all you have to do is drive there. Here is thirty thousand dollars. I will pay you the rest when you return. Then, I want you to do another job for me."

"Sure, who do I have to kill?"

"All you will be doing is planting some Angel dust on bruises ranch. I'll call in an anonymous tip to the police. They will search his ranch an arrest him and his wife for possession. Then I'll call my boss and tell him that the ranch is his."

Bruce swiftly stepped out of an unmarked car, along with a dozen police officers from other locations, hollering, "Freeze!"

Miss Greentree's two guards fired and were quickly taken down. Dug went to grab Miss Greentree, she pull a nine-millimeter from her purse, spun around pointed it at him hollering, "All of you, drop your weapons, and stand by my car or he gets a bullet in the head!" Miss Greentree, then shoved Dug towards Bruce and said, "Marshal. Your wife is about to become a widow." Before she had a chance to pull the trigger, a bullet from an unknown source struck her in the throat. She gasping for air, and fell to the street, dead. Bruce ordered, "Spread out! I want that sniper found!"

As Miss Greentree was being loaded in the ambulance, an officer reported, "Sorry Sir. We couldn't find a trace of anyone. It's as if she disappeared into thin air."

Later, Sylvia stated "Hon there is a great little steak house on West Wickenburg Way in Wickenburg, called, Charley's Steak House. We are to meet Mandy and Harry there, what do you say?"

At the Steak house, Mandy and Harry was enjoying their juicy Porterhouse Steaks, with baked potato, and string beans, when she stated, "I'll be right back. I want to see if I can have one of their menus to take home."

As Mandy was searching for the manager, Ben walked up behind her and whispered, "Don't turn around or holler, because I have a knife. Walk outside and get in my pickup."

In Ben's tan truck with a spacious cab on the back, Mandy nervously commented, "Nice Doge. Is it new?"

Ben drove out of the parking lot, turned left on West Wickenburg Way, then left on Ocotillo Drive to a dirt road called Country Line Road, and stopped the truck after driving two miles. He turned to Mandy and stated, "This is far as you go. It's time to say goodbye," and flashed his knife in her face.

Trying to stay calm, Mandy suggested, "Why don't you get a blanket from the back while I find us a nice spot outside, then you can snuggle until the cows come home." She then kicked him as hard as she could sending Ben against the truck door and sprinted off with hopes to escape. Ben jumped out of the truck, took a knife, and threw it striking Mandy in the back.

Just then, a bullet creased Ben's shoulder, he turned around and saw Harry with his Winchester pointed at him. Ben threw his hands up and said, "Mandy tried to kill me, so I had to defend myself."

Harry fired another round that grazed Ben's side and said, "That's a lie and you know it. I've been doing some checking on you and I found a long list of priors and I'd bet you are part of the drug ring here in Wickenburg."

Ben slowly bent down to tie his shoe, threw dirt in Harry's face, wrestled the rifle out of his hands and ordered him to get down on his kneed so he could shoot him.

Harry knelt down, bowed his head, and began to pray silently when a shot rang out. Harry looked up and saw Sylvia with a pistol in her hands and Ben on the ground with a bullet through his head.

Sylvia reported, "I called Patrick and he should be here any minute to tend to Mandy."

Harry rushed to Mandy's side, knelt down and said, "Hold on. Help will be here in a minute."

Harry held Mandy in his arms, she whispered, "Harry please forgive me for causing you to stumble that night."

"To be honest. I enjoyed being with you. Now, be quiet and save your strength."

Patrick dressed in hospital scrubs, drove up in a red ATV with Alexis. Hurried to Mandy and examined her. Then said, "She is alive but only by the grace of God. The ambulance will be here any minute but, I have to remove the knife." Patrick turned to his wife and said, "Alexis, get Mandy ready."

Twenty minutes later, Harry kissed Mandy and asked before she was put in the ambulance, "Would you like to go out with me when you're better?"

"Sure would."

Harry watched the ambulance until it was out of sight, turned to Patrick and questioned, "How do you manage to be where we need you so fast?"

"Oh, I have me ways. Oh, don't worry about Ben. I will have Duncan's men take care of him and his truck."

"Where are they taking Mandy?"

"Where she will get the best of care. By for now." Patrick turned to his wife and asked, "Did you make the call?"

"Sure did. But Sylvia and Harry have to leave before they get here."

Back at the ranch, Harry was clad in jeans and a red plaid shirt, sat in the gazebo with his wife who was dressed in tan shorts and a short-sleeve yellow blouse and questioned, "Who has the most to gain In forcing me off my branch? Is ruthless and doesn't care who did they kill?"

"Oh, I checked the hospital in Paula's injuries were not life-threatening."

Harry approached Bruce, clad in jeans and Jean shirt stated, "the police have a man in custody dad says he knows who the silent killer is and the one trying to force you off your property."

"Let's go see what he has to say."

"I'm coming with you," stated Sylvia.

At the police station, Harry, Bruce, and Sylvia entered a 10 by 10-foot square room with a 4 by a 4-foot gray square metal table in the center of the room. Behind the table, sat a man 35 years old with short dark brown hair clad in prison garments. Bruce inquired, "Who is it that's trying to force me off my wrench and had those young women killed to make me look bad."

"Paula Jones, you know the woman who had Sergeant Ben attack her to throw you guys off track? She then tried to seduce you, Sir, because she planned to make a bundle at selling your property to the developers."

"Are you sure it's Paula and you're not handing me some line?"

"She was the one who paid me $10,000 to beat that guy to death in the desert."

Later, Bruce rang Paula's doorbell, with his wife and Harry. Paula answered the door clad in pink hot pants in a short sleeve button down pink blouse and inquired, "long time no see what do you want?"

Bruce stated, "You are under arrest or the cheerleader murders, Miss Greentree, and one of my ranch hands."

"This has to be some type of joke. I'm no killer."

"Then you won't mind if I search your home for a sniper's rifle, and a bow and arrow."

Paula screamed, "I was willing to pay you twice the amount of money that you paid for that worthless piece of property. But no, you had to be stubborn, so I killed those cheerleaders because I thought it was a way to force you off your land plus I wanted to pay those Cheerleaders back for the way they treated me."

Paula slammed the door In Bruce's face, ran into her back bedroom, grabbed the rifle and tried to shoot Bruce but missed. Harry leveled his Winchester at her and shot her in the shoulder.

EPILOGUE

Weeks later at the campsite, eating her ham and egg breakfast, Sylvia inquired, "Sweet, did you ever find the one who killed Miss Greentree?"

"Yes, the bullet that killed Miss Greentree matched Paula's rifle. I gave Harry two months off, Because he has a chance to go to Japan on a cultural exchange. Sorry I forgot to tell you I let Barbra go before we left because I got tired of her walking in on me."

"No problem. Mandy would love the job."

"And are you going to put something more on today?"

"All I am going to do today is, set around like this, drink tea, and read my book called, 'Tara and the man. What happened to those developers that were willing to pay Paula top dollar for your land?"

"Duncan took care of them. Here are the final reports from Kitty, Connie, and Mosey. Who will be working for Duncan from now on."

"I have just one question. Paula said that her attacker wore a bra. But Ben was the one doing the killing."

"She was just putting up a smokescreen and I never get tired of seeing you like that, but, is it alright if I invite Patrick and Alexis in for a cup of coffee."

"You wouldn't dare!" stated Sylvia dropping her book and ran into the bedroom to get dressed.

Patrick entered with his wife and stated, "Bruce. I've got two ATVs outside and one of them has yours and Sylvia's names on it."

Printed in the United States
By Bookmasters